Octave Thanet

The Missionary Sheriff

Octave Thanet

The Missionary Sheriff

ISBN/EAN: 9783742894304

Manufactured in Europe, USA, Canada, Australia, Japa

Cover: Foto ©Andreas Hilbeck / pixelio.de

Manufactured and distributed by brebook publishing software
(www.brebook.com)

Octave Thanet

The Missionary Sheriff

THE MISSIONARY SHERIFF

BEING

INCIDENTS IN THE LIFE OF A PLAIN MAN
WHO TRIED TO DO HIS DUTY

BY

OCTAVE THANET

ILLUSTRATED BY

A. B. FROST AND CLIFFORD CARLETON

NEW YORK
HARPER & BROTHERS PUBLISHERS
1897

CONTENTS

ILLUSTRATIONS

THE MISSIONARY SHERIFF

THE MISSIONARY SHERIFF

SHERIFF WICKLIFF leaned out of his office window, the better to watch the boy soldiers march down the street. The huge pile of stone that is the presumed home of Justice for the county stands in the same yard with the old yellow stone jail. The court-house is ornate and imposing, although a hundred active chimneys daub its eaves and carvings, but the jail is as plain as a sledge-hammer. Yet during Sheriff Wickliff's administration, while Joe Raker kept jail and Mrs. Raker was matron, window-gardens brightened the grim walls all summer, and chrysanthemums and roses blazoned the black bars in winter.

Above the jail the street is a pretty street, with trim cottages and lawns and gardens; below, the sky-lines dwindle ignobly into shabby one and two story wooden shops devoted to the humbler handicrafts. It is not a street favored 'by processions;' only the little soldiers of the Orphans' Home Company would choose to tramp over its unkempt macadam. Good reason they had, too, since thus they passed the sheriff's office, and it was the sheriff who had given most of the money for their uniforms, and their drums and fifes outright.

A voice at the sheriff's elbow caused him to turn.

"Well, Amos," said his deputy, with Western familiarity, "getting the interest on your money ?"

Wickliff smiled as he unbent his great frame; he was six feet two inches in height, with bones and thews to match his stature. A stiff black mustache, curving about his mouth and lifting as he smiled, made his white teeth look the whiter. One of the upper teeth was crooked. That angle had come in an ugly fight (when he was a special officer and detective) in the Chicago stock - yards, he having to hold a mob at bay, single-handed, to save the life of a wounded policeman. The scar seaming his jaw and neck belonged to the time that he captured a notorious gang of train-robbers. He brought the robbers in — that is, he brought their bodies; and "That scar was worth three thousand dollars to me," he was wont to say. In point of fact it was worth more, because he had invested the money so advantageously that, thanks to it and the savings which he had been able to add, in spite of his free hand he was now become a man of property. The sheriff's high cheek-bones, straight hair (black as a dead coal), and narrow black eyes were the arguments for a general belief that an Indian ancestor lurked somewhere in the foliage of his genealogical tree. All that people really knew about him was that his mother died when he was a baby, and his father, about the same time, was killed in battle, leaving their only child to drift from one reluctant protector to another, until he brought up in the Soldiers' Orphans' Home of the State. If the sheriff's eyes were Indian, Indians may have very gentle eyes. He turned them now on the deputy with a smile.

"Well, Joe, what's up?" said he.

"The lightning-rod feller wants to see you, as soon as you come back to the jail, he says. And here's something he dropped as he was going to his room. Don't look much like it could be *his* mother. Must have prigged it."

The sheriff examined the photograph, an ordinary cabinet card. The portrait was that of a woman, pictured with the relentless frankness of a rural photographer's camera. Every sad line in the plain elderly face, every wrinkle in the ill-fitting silk gown, showed with a brutal distinctness, and somehow made the picture more pathetic. The woman's hair was gray and thin; her eyes, which were dark, looked straight forward, and seemed to meet the sheriff's gaze. They had no especial beauty of form, but they, as well as the mouth, had an expression of wistful kindliness that fixed his eyes on them for a full minute. He sighed as he dropped his hand. Then he observed that there was writing on the reverse side of the carte, and lifted it again to read.

In a neat cramped hand was written:

"To Eddy, from Mother.   *Feb.* 21, 1889.
"The Lord bless thee and keep thee. The Lord make His face to shine upon thee, and be gracious unto thee; the Lord lift up His countenance upon thee, and give thee peace."

Wickliff put the carte in his pocket.

"That's just the kind of mother I'd like to have," said he; "awful nice and good, and not so fine she'd be ashamed of me. And to think of *him!*"

"He's an awful slick one," assented the deputy, cordially. "Two years we've been ayfter him. New games all the time; but the lightning-rods ain't in it with this last scheme—working hisself off as a Methodist parson on the road to a job, and stopping all night, and then the runaway couple happening in, and that poor farmer and his wife so excited and interested, and of course they'd witness and sign the certificate; wisht I'd seen them when they found out!"

"They gave 'em cake and some currant wine, too."

"That's just like women. Say, I didn't think the girl was much to brag on for looks—"

"Got a kinder way with her, though," Wickliff struck in. "Depend on it, Joseph, the most dangerous of them all are the homely girls with a way to them. A man's off his guard with them; he's sorry for them not being pretty, and being so nice and humble; and before he knows it they're winding him 'round their finger."

"I didn't know you was so much of a philosopher, Amos," said the deputy, admiring him.

"It ain't me, Joe; it's the business. Being a philosopher, I take it, ain't much more than seeing things with the paint off; and there's nothing like being a detective to get the paint off. It's a great business for keeping a man straight, too, seeing the consequences of wickedness so constantly, especially fool wickedness that gets found out. Well, Joe, if this lady"—touching his breast pocket—"is that guy's mother, I'm awful sorry for her, for I know she tried to train him right. I'll go over and find out, I guess."

So saying, and quite unconscious of the approving looks of his subordinate (for he was a simple-minded, modest man, who only spoke out of the fulness of his heart), the sheriff walked over to the jail.

The corridor into which the cells of the unconvicted prisoners opened was rather full to-day. As the sheriff entered, every one greeted him, even the sullen-browed man talking with a sobbing woman through the bars, and every one smiled. He nodded to all, but only spoke to the visitor. He said, "I guess he didn't do it this time, Lizzie; he won't be in long."

"That's what I bin tellin' her," growled the man, "and she won't believe me; I told her I promised you—"

"And God A'mighty bless you, sheriff, for what you done!" the woman wailed. The sheriff had some ado to escape from her benedictions politely; but he got away, and knocked at the door of the last cell on the tier. The inmate opened the door himself.

He was a small man, who still was wearing the clerical habit of his last criminal masquerade;

and his face carried out the suggestion of his costume, being an actor's face, not only in the clean-shaven cheeks and lips, but in the flexibility of the features and the unconscious alertness of gaze. He was fair of skin, and his light-brown hair was worn off his head at the temples. His eyes were fine, well shaped, of a beautiful violet color, and an extremely pleasant expression. He looked like a mere boy across the room in the shadow, but as he advanced, certain deep lines about his mouth displayed themselves and raised his age. The sunlight showed that he was thin; he was haggard the instant he ceased to smile. With a very good manner he greeted the sheriff, to whom he proffered the sole chair of the apartment.

"Guess the bed will hold me," said the sheriff, testing his words by sitting down on the white-covered iron bedstead. "Well, I hear you wanted to see me."

"Yes, sir. I want to get my money that you took away from me."

"Well, I guess you can't have it." The sheriff spoke with a smile, but his black eyes narrowed a little. "I guess the court will have to decide first if that ain't old man Goodrich's money that you got from the note he supposed was a marriage certificate. I guess you better not put any hopes on that money, Mr. Paisley. Wasn't that the name you gave me?"

"Paisley 'll do," said the other man, indifferently. "What became of my friend?"

"The sheriff of Hardin County wanted the man, and the lady—well, the lady is here boarding with me."

"Going to squeal?"

"Going to tell all she knows."

Paisley's hand went up to his mouth; he changed color. "It's like her," he muttered—"oh, it's just like her!" And he added a villanous epithet.

"None of that talk," said Wickliff.

The man had jumped up and was pacing his narrow space, fighting against a climbing rage. "You see," he cried, unable to contain himself —"you see, what makes me so mad is now I've got to get my mother to help me—and I'd rather take a licking!".

"I should think you would," said Wickliff, dryly. "Say, this your mother?" He handed him the photograph, the written side upward.

"It came in a Bible," explained Paisley, with an embarrassed air.

"Your mother rich?"

"She can raise the money."

"Meaning, I expect, that she can mortgage

her house and lot. Look here, Smith, this ain't
the first time your ma has sent you money, but
if I was you I'd have the last time *stay* the last.
She don't look equal to much more hard work."

"My name's Paisley, if you please," returned
the prisoner, stolidly, "and I can take care of
my own mother. If she's lent me money I have
paid it back. This is only for bail, to deposit—"

"There is the chance," interrupted Wickliff,
"of your skipping. Now, I tell you, I like the
looks of your mother, and I don't mean she shall
run any risks. So, if you do get money from her,
I shall personally look out you don't forfeit your
bail. Besides, court is in session now, so the
chances are you wouldn't more than get the
money before it would be your turn. See ?"

"Anyhow I've got to have a lawyer."

"Can't see why, young feller. I'll give you a
straight tip. There ain't enough law in Iowa to
get you out of this scrape. We've got the cinch
on you, and there ain't any possible squirming
out."

"So you say ;" the sneer was a little forced ;
"I've heard of your game before. Nice, kind
officers, ready to advise a man and pump him
dry, and witness against him afterwards. I ain't
that kind of a sucker, Mr. Sheriff."

"Nor I ain't that kind of an officer, Mr. Smith.

You'd ought to know about my reputation by
this time."

"They say you're square," the prisoner admitted ; "but you ain't so stuck on me as to
care a damn whether I go over the road ; expect
you'd want to send me for the trouble I've given
you," and he grinned. "Well, what *are* you
after ?"

"Helping your mother, young feller. I had
a mother myself."

"It ain't uncommon."

"Maybe a mother like mine—and yours—is,
though."

The prisoner's eyes travelled down to the face
on the carte. "That's right," he said, with another ring in his voice. "I wouldn't mind half
so much if I could keep my going to the pen from
her. She's never found out about me."

"How much family you got ?" said Wickliff,
thoughtfully.

"Just a mother. I ain't married. There was
a girl, my sister—good sort too, 'nuff better'n
me. She used to be a clerk in the store, type-
writer, bookkeeper, general utility, you know.
My position in the first place ; and when I—well,
resigned, they gave it to her. She helped mother buy the place. Two years ago she died. You
may believe me or not, but I would have gone

back home then and run straight if it hadn't
been for Mame. I would, by —— ! I had five
hundred dollars then, and I was going back to
give every damned cent of it to ma, tell her to
put it into the bakery—"

"That how she makes a living ?"

"Yes—little two-by-four bakery—oh, I'm giving you straight goods—makes pies and cakes
and bread—good, too, you bet—makes it herself.
Ruth Graves, who lives round the corner, comes
in and helps—keeps the books, and tends shop
busy times; tends the oven too, I guess. She
was a great friend of Ellie's—and mine. She's
a real good girl. Well, I didn't get mother's
letters till it was too late, and I felt bad; I had
a mind to go right down to Fairport and go in
with ma. That—*she* stopped it. Got me off on
a tear somehow, and by the time I was sober
again the money was 'most all gone. I sent what
was left off to ma, and I went on the road again
myself. But she's the devil."

"That the time you hit her ?"

The prisoner nodded. "Oughtn't to, of course.
Wasn't brought up that way. My father was a
Methodist preacher, and a good one. But I tell
you the coons that say you never must hit a
woman don't know anything about that sort of
women ; there ain't nothing on earth so infernal-

ly exasperating as a woman. They can mad you worse than forty men."

It was the sheriff's turn to nod, which he did gravely, with even a glimmer of sympathy in his mien.

"Well, she never forgave you," said he; "she's had it in for you since."

"And she knows I won't squeal, 'cause I'd have to give poor Ben away," said the prisoner; "but I tell you, sheriff, she was at the bottom of the deviltry every time, and she managed to bag the best part of the swag, too."

"I dare say. Well, to come back to business, the question with you is how to keep these here misfortunes of yours from your mother, ain't it?"

"Of course."

"Well, the best plan for you is to plead guilty, showing you don't mean to give the court any more trouble. Tell the judge you are sick of your life, and going to quit. You are, ain't you?" the sheriff concluded, simply; and the swindler, after an instant's hesitation, answered:

"Damned if I won't, if I can get a job!"

"Well, that admitted"—the sheriff smoothed his big knees gently as he talked, his mild attentive eyes fixed on the prisoner's nervous presence—"that admitted, best plan is for you to plead guilty, and maybe we can fix it so's you will be sentenced to jail instead of the pen. Then we can keep it from your mother easy. Write her you've got a job here in this town, and have your letters sent to my care. I'll get you something to do. She'll never suspect that you are the notorious Ned Paisley. And it ain't likely you go home often enough to make not going awkward."

"I haven't been home in four years. But see here · how long am I likely to get ?"

The sheriff looked at him, at the hollow cheeks and sunken eyes and narrow chest—all so cruelly declared in the sunshine ; and unconsciously he modulated his voice when he spoke.

"I wouldn't worry about that, if I was you. You need a rest. You are run down pretty low. You ain't rugged enough for the life you've been leading."

The prisoner's eyes strayed past the grating to the green hills and the pleasant gardens, where some children were playing. The sheriff did not move. There was as little sensibility in his impassive mask as in a wooden Indian's ; but behind the trained apathy was a real compassion. He was thinking. "The boy don't look like he had a year's life in him. I bet he knows it himself. And when he stares that way out of the window he's thinking he ain't never going to be foot-loose in the sun again. Kinder tough, I call it."

The young man's eyes suddenly met his. "Well, it's no great matter, I guess," said he. "I'll do it. But I can't for the life of me make out why you are taking so much trouble."

He was surprised at Wickliff's reply. It was, "Come on down stairs with me, and I'll show you."

"You mean it?"

"Yes; go ahead."

"You want my parole not to cut and run?"

"Just as you like about that. Better not try any fooling."

The prisoner uttered a short laugh, glancing from his own puny limbs to the magnificent muscles of the officer.

"Straight ahead, after you're out of the corridor, down-stairs, and turn to the right," said Wickliff.

Silently the prisoner followed his directions, and when they had descended the stairs and turned to the right, the sheriff's hand pushed beneath his elbow and opened the door before them. "My rooms," said Wickliff. "Being a single man, it's handier for me living in the jail." The rooms were furnished with the unchastened gorgeousness of a Pullman sleeper, the brilliant hues of a Brussels carpet on the floor, blue plush at the windows and on the chairs. The walls were hung with the most expensive gilt paper that the town could furnish (after all, it was a modest price per roll), and against the gold, photographs of the district judges assumed a sinister dignity. There was also a photograph of the court-house, and one of the jail, and a model in bas-relief of the Capitol at Des Moines ; but more prominent than any of these were two portraits opposite the windows. They were oil-paintings, elaborately framed, and they had cost so much that the sheriff rested happily content that they must be well painted. Certainly the artist had not recorded impressions ; rather he seemed to have worked with a microscope, not slighting an eyelash. One of the portraits was that of a stiff and stern young man in a soldier's uniform. He was dark, and had eyes and feat-ures like the sheriff. The other was the portrait of a young girl. In the original daguerreotype from which the artist worked the face was come-ly, if not pretty, and the innocence in the eyes and the timid smile made it winning. The ar-tist had enlarged the eyes and made the mouth smaller, and bestowed (with the most amiable in-tentions) a complexion of hectic brilliancy ; but there still remained, in spite of paint, a flicker of

2

the old touching expression. Between the two canvases hung a framed letter. It was labelled in bold Roman script, "Letter of Capt. R. T. Manley," and a glance showed the reader that it was the description of a battle to a friend. One sentence was underlined. "We also lost Private A. T. Wickliff, killed in the charge—a good man who could always be depended on to do his duty."

The sheriff guided his bewildered visitor opposite these portraits and lifted his hand above the other's shoulder. "You see them?" said he. "They're *my* father and mother. You see that letter? It was wrote by my father's old captain and sent to me. What he says about my father is everything that I know. But it's enough. He was 'a good man who could always be depended on to do his duty.' You can't say no more of the President of the United States. I've had a pretty tough time of it in my own life, as a man's got to have who takes up my line; but I've tried to live so my father needn't be ashamed of me. That other picture is my mother. I don't know nothing about her, nothing at all; and I don't need to—except those eyes of hers. There's a look someway about your mother's eyes like mine. Maybe it's only the look one good woman has like another; but whatever it is, your mother made me think of mine. She's the kind of mother I'd like to have; and if I can help it, she sha'n't know her son's in the penitentiary. Now come on back."

As silently as he had gone, the prisoner followed the sheriff back to his cell. "Good-bye, Paisley," said the sheriff, at the door.

"Good-bye, sir; I'm much obliged," said the prisoner. Not another word was said.

That evening, however, good Mrs. Raker told the sheriff that, to her mind, if ever a man was struck with death, that new young fellow was; and he had been crying, too; his eyes were all red.

"He needs to cry," was all the comfort that the kind soul received from the sheriff, the cold remark being accompanied by what his·familiars called his Indian scowl.

Nevertheless, he did his utmost for the prisoner as a quiet intercessor, and his merciful prophecy was accomplished — Edgar S. Paisley was permitted to serve out his sentence in the jail instead of the State prison. His state of health had something to do with the judge's clemency, and the sheriff could not but suspect that, in his own phrase, "Paisley played his cough and his hollow cheeks for all they were worth."

"But that's natural," he observed to Raker, "and he's doing it partially for the old lady. Well, I'll try to give her a quiet spell."

"Yes," Raker responds, dubiously, "but he'll be at his old games the minute he gits out."

"You don't suppose"—the sheriff speaks with a certain embarrassment—"you don't suppose there'd be any chance of really reforming him, so as he'd stick ?—he ain't likely to live long."

"Nah," says the unbelieving deputy ; "he's a deal too slick to be reformed."

The sheriff's pucker of his black brows and his slow nod might have meant anything. Really he was saying to himself (Amos was a dogged fellow) : "Don't care ; I'm going to try. I am sure ma would want me to. I ain't a very hefty missionary, but if there is such a thing as clubbing a man half-way decent, and I think there is, I'll get him that way. Poor old lady, she looked so unhappy !"

During the trial Paisley was too excited and dejected to write to his mother. But the day after he received his sentence the sheriff found him finishing a large sheet of foolscap.

It contained a detailed and vivid description of the reasons why he had left a mythical grocery firm, and described with considerable humor the mythical boarding-house where he was waiting for something to turn up. It was very well done, and he expected a smile from the sheriff. The red mottled his pale cheeks when Wickliff, with

"TORE THE LETTER INTO PIECES"

his blackest frown, tore the letter into pieces, which he stuffed into his pocket.

"You take a damned ungentlemanly advantage of your position," fumed Paisley.

"I shall take more advantage of it if you give me any sass," returned Wickliff, calmly. "Now set down and listen." Paisley, after one helpless glare, did sit down. "I believe you fairly revel in lying. I don't. That's where we differ. I think lies are always liable to come home to roost, and I like to have the flock as small as possible. Now you write that you are here, and you're helping *me*. You ain't getting much wages, but they will be enough to keep you—these hard times any job is better than none. And you can add that you don't want any money .from her. Your other letter sorter squints like you did. You can say you are boarding with a very nice lady—that's Mrs. Raker—everything very clean, and the table plain but abundant. Address you in care of Sheriff Amos T. Wickliff. How's that?"

Paisley's anger had ebbed away. Either from policy or some other motive he was laughing now. "It's not nearly so interesting in a literary point of view, you know," said he, "but I guess it will be easier not to have so many things to remember. And you're right; I didn't mean to hint for money, but it did look like it."

"He did mean to hint," thought the sheriff, "but he's got some sense." The letter finally submitted was a masterpiece in its way. This time the sheriff smiled, though grimly. He also gave Paisley a cigar.

Regularly the letters to Mrs. Smith were submitted to Wickliff. Raker never thought of reading them. The replies came with a pathetic promptness. "That's from your ma," said Wickliff, when the first letter came—Paisley was at the jail ledgers in the sheriff's room, as it happened, directly beneath the portraits—"you better read it first."

Paisley read it twice; then he turned and handed it to the sheriff, with a half apology. "My mother talks a good deal better than she writes. Women are naturally interested in petty things, you know. Besides, I used to be fond of the old dog; that's why she writes so much about him."

"I have a dog myself," growled the sheriff. "Your mother writes a beautiful letter." His eyes were already travelling down the cheap thin note-paper, folded at the top. "I know," Mrs. Smith wrote, in her stiff, careful hand—"I know you will feel bad, Eddy, to hear that dear old

Rowdy is gone. Your letter came the night before he died. Ruth was over, and I read it out
loud to her ; and when I came to that part where
you sent your love to him, it seemed like he
understood, he wagged his tail so knowing. You
know how fond of you he always was. All that
evening he played round—more than usual—and
I'm so glad we both petted him, for in the morning we found him stiff and cold on the landing
of the stairs, in his favorite place. I don't think
he could have suffered any, he looked so peaceful. Ruth and I made a grave for him in the
garden, under the white rose tree. Ruth digged
the grave, and she painted a Kennedy's cracker-
box, and we wrapped him up in white cotton
cloth. I cried, and Ruth cried too, when we
laid him away. Somehow it made me long so
much more to see you. If I sent you the money,
don't you think you could come home for Christmas ? Wouldn't your employer let you if he
knew your mother had not seen you for four
years, and you are all the child she has got?
But I don't want you to neglect your business."

The few words of affection that followed were
not written so firmly as the rest. The sheriff
would not read them ; he handed the letter back
to Paisley, and turned his Indian scowl on the
back of the latter's shapely head.

Paisley was staring at the columns of the page before him. "Rowdy was my dog when I was courting Ruth," he said. "I was engaged to her once. I suppose mother thinks of that. Poor Rowdy! the night I ran away he followed me, and I had to whip him back."

"Oh, you ran away?"

"Oh yes; the old story. Trusted clerk. Meant to return the money. It wasn't very much. But it about cleaned mother out. Then she started the bakery."

"You pay your ma back?"

"Yes, I did."

"That's a lie."

"What do you ask a man such questions for, then? Do you think it's pleasant admitting what a dirty dog you've been? Oh, damn you!"

"You do see it, then," said the sheriff, in a very pleasant, gentle tone; "that's one good thing. For you have *got* to reform, Ned; I'm going to give your mother a decent boy. Well, what happened then? Girl throw you over?"

"Why, I ran straight for a while," said Paisley, furtively wiping first one eye and then the other with a finger; "there wasn't any scandal. Ruth stuck by me, and a married sister of hers (who didn't know) got her husband to give me a place. I was doing all right, and—and sending home money to ma, and I would have been all right now, if—if—I hadn't met Mame, and she made a crazy fool of me. Then Ruth shook me. Oh, I ain't blaming her! It was hearing about Mame. But after that I just went a-flying to the devil. Now you know why I wanted to see Mame."

"You wanted to kill her," said the sheriff, "or you think you did. But you couldn't; she'd have talked you over. Still, I thought I wouldn't risk it. You know she's gone now?"

"I supposed she'd be, now the trial's over." In a minute he added: "I'm glad I didn't touch her; mother would have had to know that. Look here; how am I going to get over that invitation?"

"I'll trust you for that lie," said Wickliff, sauntering off.

Paisley wrote that he would not take his mother's money. When he could come home on his own money he would gladly. He wrote a long affectionate letter, which the sheriff read, and handed back with the dry comment, "That will do, I guess."

But he gave Paisley a brier-wood pipe and a pound of Yale Mixture that afternoon.

The correspondence threw some side-lights on Paisley's past.

"You've got to write your ma every week," announced Wickliff, when the day came round.

"Why, I haven't written once a month."

"Probably not, but you have got to write once a week now. Your mother 'll get used to it. I should think you'd be glad to do the only thing you can for the mother that's worked her fingers off for you."

"I *am* glad," said Paisley, sullenly.

He never made any further demur. He wrote very good letters; and more and more, as the time passed, he grew interested in the correspondence. Meanwhile he began to acquire (quite unsuspected by the sheriff) a queer respect for that personage. The sheriff was popular among the prisoners; perhaps the general sentiment was voiced by one of them, who exclaimed, one day, after his visit, "Well, I never did see a man as had killed so many men put on so little airs!"

Paisley began his acquaintance with a contempt for the slow-moving intellect that he attributed to his sluggish-looking captor. He felt the superiority of his own better education. It was grateful to his vanity to sneer in secret at Wickliff's slips in grammar or information. And presently he had opportunity to indulge his humor in this respect, for Wickliff began lend-

ing him books. The jail library, as a rule, was
managed by Mrs. Raker. She was, she used to
say, "a great reader," and dearly loved "a nice
story that made you cry all the way through and
ended right." Her taste was catholic in fiction
(she never read anything else), and her favorites
were Mrs. Southworth, Charles Dickens, and
Walter Scott. The sheriff's own reading seldom
strayed beyond the daily papers, but with the
aid of a legal friend he had selected some stand-
ard biographies and histories to add to the singular conglomeration of fiction and religion sent
to the jail by a charitable public. On Paisley's
request for reading, the sheriff went to Mrs.
Raker. She promptly pulled *Ishmael Worth, or
Out of the Depths,* from the shelf. "It's beautiful," says she, "and when he gits through with
that he can have the *Pickwick Papers* to cheer
him up. Only I kinder hate to lend that book
to the prisoners; there's so much about good
eatin' in it, it makes 'em dissatisfied with the
table."

"He's got to have something improving, too,"
says the sheriff. "I guess the history of the
United States will do; you've read the others,
and know they're all right. I'll run through
this."

He told Paisley the next morning that he had

sat up almost all night reading, he was so afraid that enough of the thirteen States wouldn't ratify the Constitution. This was only one of the artless comments that tickled Paisley. Yet he soon began to notice the sheriff's keenness of observation, and a kind of work-a-day sense that served him well. He fell to wondering, during those long nights when his cough kept him awake, whether his own brilliant and subtle ingenuity had done as much for him. He could hardly tell the moment of its beginning, but he began to value the approval of this big, ignorant, clumsy, strong man.

Insensibly he grew to thinking of conduct more in the sheriff's fashion ; and his letters not only reflected the change in his moral point of view, they began to have more and more to say of the sheriff. Very soon the mother began to be pathetically thankful to this good friend of her boy, whose habits were so correct, whose influence so admirable. In her grateful happiness over the frequent letters and their affection were revealed the unexpressed fears that had tortured her for years. She asked for Wickliff's picture. Paisley did not know that the sheriff had a photograph taken on purpose. Mrs. Smith pronounced him "a handsome man." To be sure, the unscarred side of his face was taken. "He looks firm, too," wrote the poor mother, whose own boy had never known how to be firm; "I think he must be a Daniel."

"A which?" exclaimed the puzzled Daniel.

"Didn't you ever go to Sunday-school? Don't you know the verses,

> "'Dare to be a Daniel;
> Dare to make a stand'?"

The sheriff's reply was enigmatical. It was: "Well, to think of you having such a mother as that!"

"I don't deserve her, that's a fact," said Paisley, with his flippant air. "And yet, would you believe it, I used to be the model boy of the Sunday-school. Won all the prizes. Ma's got them in a drawer."

"Dare say. They thought you were a awful good boy, because you always kept your face clean and brushed your hair without being told to, and learned your lessons quick, and always said 'Yes, 'm,' and 'No, 'm,' and when you got into a scrape lied out of it, and picked up bad habits as easy and quiet as a long-haired dog catches fleas. Oh, I know your sort of model boy! We had 'em at the Orphans' Home; I've taken their lickings, too."

Paisley's thin face was scarlet before the speech

was finished. "Some of that is true," said he; "but at least I never hit a fellow when he was down."

The sheriff narrowed his eyes in a way that he had when thinking; he put both hands in his pockets and contemplated Paisley's irritation. "Well, young feller, you have some reason to talk that way to me," said he. "The fact is, I was mad at you, thinking about your mother. I —I respect that lady very highly."

Paisley forced a feeble smile over his "So do I."

But after this episode the sheriff's manner visibly softened to the young man. He told Raker that there were good spots in Paisley.

"Yes, he's mighty slick," said Raker.

Thanksgiving - time, a box from his mother came to the prisoner, and among the pies and cakes was an especial pie for Mr. Wickliff, "From his affectionate old friend, Rebecca Smith."

The sheriff spent fully two hours communing with a large new *Manual of Etiquette and Correspondence;* then he submitted a letter to Paisley. Paisley read :

"DEAR MADAM,—Your favor (of the pie) of the 24th inst. is received and I beg you to accept my sincere and warm thanks. Ned is an efficient clerk and his habits

THE THANKSGIVING BOX

are very correct. We are reading history, in our leisure
hours. We have read Fisk's Constitutional History of
the United States and two volumes of Macaulay's History
of England. Both very interesting books. I think that
Judge Jeffreys was the meanest and worst judge I ever
heard of. My early education was not as extensive as I
could wish, and I am very glad of the valuable assistance
which I receive from your son. He is doing well and
sends his love. Hoping, my dear Madam, to be able to see
you and thank you personally for your very kind and welcome gift, I am, with respect,

"Very Truly Yours,

"Amos T. Wickliff."

Paisley read the letter soberly. In fact, another feeling destroyed any inclination to smile
over the unusual pomp of Wickliff's style.
"That's out of sight!" he declared. "It will
please the old lady to the ground. Say, I take
it very kindly of you, Mr. Wickliff, to write
about me that way."

"I had a book to help me," confessed the flat-
tered sheriff. "And — say, Paisley, when you
are writing about me to your ma, you better say
Wickliff, or Amos. Mr. Wickliff sounds kinder
stiff. I'll understand."

The letter that the sheriff received in return
he did not show to Paisley. He read it with a
knitted brow, and more than once he brushed
his hand across his eyes. When he finished it

he drew a long sigh, and walked up to his mother's portrait. "She says she prays for me every night, ma"—he spoke under his breath, and reverently. "Ma, I simply have *got* to save that boy for her, haven't I ?"

That evening Paisley rather timidly approached a subject which he had tried twice before to broach, but his courage had failed him. "You said something, Mr. Wickliff, of paying me a little extra for what I do, keeping the books, etc. Would you mind telling me what it will be ? I —I'd like to send a Christmas present to my mother."

"That's right," said the sheriff, heartily. "I was thinking what would suit her. How's a nice black dress, and a bill pinned to it to pay for making it up ?"

"But I never—"

"You can pay me when you get out."

"Do you think I'll ever get out ?" Paisley's fine eyes were fixed on Wickliff as he spoke, with a sudden wistful eagerness. He had never alluded to his health before, yet it had steadily failed. Now he would not let Amos answer; he may have flinched from any confirmation of his own fears; he took the word hastily. "Anyhow, you'll risk my turning out a bad investment. But you'll do a damned kind ac-tion to my mother; and if I'm a rip, she's a saint."

"*Sure*," said the sheriff. "Say, do you think she'd mind my sending her a hymn-book and a few flowers ?"

Thus it came to pass that the tiny bakery window, one Christmas-day, showed such a crimson glory of roses as the village had never seen; and the widow Smith, bowing her shabby black bonnet on the pew rail, gave thanks and tears for a happy Christmas, and prayed for her son's friend. She prayed for her son also, that he might " be kept good." She felt that her prayer would be answered. God knows, perhaps it was.

That night before she went to bed she wrote to Edgar and to Amos. " I am writing to both my boys," she said to Amos, " for I feel like *you* were my dear son too."

When Amos answered this letter he did not consult the Manual. It was one day in January, early in the month, that he received the first bit of encouragement for his missionary work palpable enough to display to the scoffer Raker. Yet it was not a great thing either; only this: Paisley (already half an hour at work in the sheriff's room) stopped, fished from his sleeve a piece of note-paper folded into the measure of a knife-blade, and offered it to the sheriff.

3

"See what Mame sent me," said he; "just read it."

There was a page of it, the purport being that the writer had done what she had through jealousy, which she knew now was unfounded; she was suffering indescribable agonies from remorse; and, to prove she meant what she said, if her darling Ned would forgive her she would get him out before a week was over. If he agreed he was to be at his window at six o'clock Wednesday night. The day was Thursday.

"How did you get this?" asked Amos. "Do you mind telling?"

"Not the least. It came in a coat. From Barber & Glasson's. The one Mrs. Raker picked out for me, and it was sent up from the store. She got at it somehow, I suppose."

"But how did you get word where to look?"

Paisley grinned. "Mame was here, visiting that fellow who was taken up for smashing a window, and pretended he was so hungry he had to have a meal in jail. Mame put him up to it, so she could come. She gave me the tip where to look then."

"I see. I got on to some of those signals once. Well, did you show yourself Wednesday?"

"Not much!" He hesitated, and did not look

at the sheriff, scrawling initials on the blotting-pad with his pen. "Did you really think, Mr. Wickliff, after all you've done for me—and my mother—I would go back on you and get you into trouble for that—"

"'S-sh! Don't call names!" Wickliff looked apprehensively at the picture of his mother. "Why didn't you give me this before?"

"Because you weren't here till this morning. I wasn't going to give it to Raker."

"What do you suppose she's after?"

"Oh, she's got some big scheme on foot, and she needs me to work it. I'm sick of her. I'm sick of the whole thing. I want to run straight. I want to be the man my poor mother thinks I am."

"And I want to help you, Ned," cried the sheriff. For the first time he caught the other's hand and wrung it.

"I guess the Lord wants to help me too," said Paisley, in a queer dry tone.

"Why—yes—of course he wants to help all of us," said the sheriff, embarrassed. Then he frowned, and his voice roughened as he asked, "What do you mean by that?"

"Oh, you know what I mean," said Paisley, smiling; "you've always known it. It's been getting worse lately. I guess I caught cold.

Some mornings I have to stop two or three times
when I dress myself, I have such fits of cough-
ing."

"Why didn't you tell, and go to the hospital?"

"I wanted to come down here. It's so pleasant down here."

"Good—" The sheriff reined his tongue in
time, and only said, "Look here, you've got to
see a doctor!"

Therefore the encouragement to the missionary work was embittered by divers conflicting
feelings. Even Raker was disturbed when the
doctor announced that Paisley had pneumonia.

"Double pneumonia and a slim chance, of
course," gloomed Raker. "Always so. Can't
have a man git useful and be a little decent, but
he's got to die! Why couldn't it 'a' been that
tramp tried to set the jail afire?"

"What I'm a-thinking of is his poor ma, who
used to write him such beautiful letters," said
Mrs. Raker, wiping her kind eyes. "They was
so attached. Never a week he didn't write her."

"It's his mother I'm thinking of, too," said
the sheriff, with a groan; "she'll be wanting to
come and see him, and how in—" He swallowed
an agitated oath, and paced the floor, his hands
clasped behind him, his lip under his teeth, and
his blackest Indian scowl on his brow—plain

signs to all who knew him that he was fighting his way through some mental thicket.

But he had never looked gentler than he looked an hour later, as he stepped softly into Paisley's cell. Mrs. Raker was holding a foaming glass to the sick man's lips. "There; take another sup of the good nog," she said, coaxingly, as one talks to a child.

"No, thank you, ma'am," said Paisley. "Queer how I've thought so often how I'd like the taste of whiskey again on my tongue, and now I can have all I want, I don't care a hooter!"

His voice was rasped in the chords, and he caught his breath between his sentences. Forty-eight hours had made an ugly alteration in his face; the eyes were glassy, the features had shrunken in an indescribable, ghastly way, and the fair skin was of a yellowish pallor, with livid circles about the eyes and the open mouth.

Wickliff greeted him, assuming his ordinary manner. They shook hands.

"There's one thing, Mr. Wickliff," said Paisley: "you'll keep this from my mother. She'd worry like blazes, and want to come here."

There was a photograph on the table, propped up by books; the sheriff's hand was on it, and he moved it, unconsciously: "'To Eddy, from Mother. The Lord bless and keep thee. The

Lord make his face to shine upon thee, and be gracious unto thee—'" Wickliff cleared his throat. "Well, I don't know, Ned," he said, cheerfully; "maybe that would be a good thing —kind of brace you up and make you get well quicker."

Mrs. Raker noticed nothing in his voice; but Paisley rolled his eyes on the impassive face in a strange, quivering, searching look; then he closed them and feebly turned his head.

"Don't you want me to telegraph? Don't you want to see her?"

Some throb of excitement gave Paisley the strength to lift himself up on the pillows. "What do you want to rile me all up for?" His voice was almost a scream. "Want to see her? It's the only thing in this damned fool world I do want! But I can't have her know; it would kill her to know. You must make up some lie about it's being diphtheria and awful sudden, and no time for her to come, and have me all out of the way before she gets here. You've been awful good to me, and you can do anything you like; it's the last I'll bother you— don't let her find out!"

"For the land's sake!" sniffed Mrs. Raker, in tears—"don't she know?"

"No, ma'am, she don't; and she never will,

either," said the sheriff. " There, Ned, boy, you lay right down. I'll fix it. And you shall see her, too. I'll fix it."

" Yes, he'll fix it. Amos will fix it. Don't you worry," sobbed Mrs. Raker, who had not the least idea how the sheriff could arrange matters, but was just as confident that he would as if the future were unrolled before her gaze.

The prisoner breathed a long deep sigh of relief, and patted the strong hand at his shoulder. And Amos gently laid him back on the pillows.

Before nightfall Paisley was lying in Amos Wickliff's own bed, while Amos, at his side, was critically surveying both chamber and parlor under half-closed eyelids. He was trying to see them with the eyes of the elderly widow of a Methodist minister.

"Hum—yes !" The result of the survey was, on the whole, satisfactory. "All nice, high-toned, first-class pictures. Nothing to shock a lady. Liquors all put away, 'cept what's needed for him. Pops all put away, so she won't be finding one and be killing herself, thinking it's not loaded. My bed moved in here comfortable for him, because he thought it was such a pleasant room, poor boy. Another bed in my room for her. Bath-room next door, hot and cold water. Little gas stove. Trained nurse who doesn't know anything, and so can't tell. Thinks it's my friend Smith. *Is* there anything else ?"

At this moment the white counterpane on the bed stirred.

" Well, Ned ?" said Wickliff.

" It's—nice !" said Paisley.

" 'That's right. Now you get a firm grip on what I'm going to say—such a grip you won't lose it, even if you get out of your head a little."

" I won't," said Paisley.

" All right. You're not Paisley any more. You're Ned Smith. I've had you moved here into my rooms because your boarding-place wasn't so good. Everybody here understands, and has got their story ready. The nurse thinks you're my friend Smith. You are, too, and you are to call me Amos. The telegram's gone. 'S-sh !—what a way to do !"—for Paisley was crying. " Ain't I her boy too ?"

One weak place remained in the fortress that Amos had builded against prying eyes and chattering tongues. He had searched in vain for " Mame." There was no especial reason, except pure hatred and malice, to dread her going to Paisley's mother, but the sheriff had enough knowledge of Mame's kind to take these qualities into account.

From the time that Wickliff promised him

that he should have his mother, Paisley seemed to be freed from every misgiving. He was too ill to talk much, and much of the time he was miserably occupied with his own suffering; yet often during the night and day before she came he would lift his still beautiful eyes to Mrs. Raker's and say, " It's to-morrow night ma comes, isn't it ?" To which the soft-hearted woman would sometimes answer, " Yes, son," and sometimes only work her chin and put her handkerchief to her eyes. Once she so far forgot the presence of the gifted professional nurse that she sniffed aloud, whereupon that personage administered a scorching tonic, in the guise of a glance, and poor Mrs. Raker went out of the room and cried.

He must have kept some reckoning of the time, for the next day he varied his question. He said, " It's to-day she's coming, isn't it ?" As the day wore on, the customary change of his disease came : he was relieved of his worst pain ; he thought that he was better. So thought Mrs. Raker and the sheriff. The doctor and the nurse maintained their inscrutable professional calm. At ten o'clock the sheriff (who had been gone for a half-hour) softly opened the door. The sick man instantly roused. He half sat up. " I know," he exclaimed ; " it's ma. Ma's come !"

The nurse rose, ready to protect her patient.

There entered a little, black-robed, gray-haired woman, who glided swift as a thought to the bedside, and gathered the worn young head to her breast. "My boy, my dear, good boy!" she said, under her breath, so low the nurse did not hear her; she only heard her say, "Now you must get well."

"Oh, I *am* glad, ma!" said the sick man.

After that the nurse was well content with them all. They obeyed her implicitly. It was she rather than Mrs. Raker who observed that Mr. Smith's mother was not alone, but accompanied by a slim, fair, brown-eyed young woman, who lingered in the background, and would fain have not spoken to the invalid at all had she not been gently pushed forward by the mother, with the words, "And Ruth came too, Eddy!"

"Thank you, Ruth; I knew that you wouldn't let ma come alone," said Ned, feebly.

The young woman had opened her lips. Now they closed. She looked at him compassionately. "Surely not, Ned," she said.

But why, wondered the nurse, who was observant—it was her trade to observe—why did she look at him so intently, and with such a shocked pity?

Ned did not express much—the sick, especially the very sick, cannot; but whenever he waked in the night and saw his mother bending over him he smiled happily, and she would answer his thought. "Yes, my boy; my dear, good boy," she would say.

And the sheriff in his dim corner thought sadly that the ruined life would always be saved for her now, and her son would be her good boy forever. Yet he muttered to himself, "I suppose the Lord is helping me out, and I ought to feel obliged, but I'm hanged if I wouldn't rather take the chances and have the boy get well!"

But he knew all the time that there was no hope for Ned's life. He lived three days after his mother came. The day before his death he was alone for a short time with the sheriff, and asked him to be good to his mother. "Ruth will be good to her too," he said; "but last night I dreamed Mame was chasing mother, and it scared me. You won't let her get at mother, will you?"

"Of course I won't," said the sheriff; "we're watching your mother every minnit; and if that woman comes here, Raker has orders to clap her in jail. And I will always look out for your ma, Ned, and she never shall know."

"That's good," said Ned, in his feeble voice. "I'll tell you something: I always wanted to be good, but I was always bad ; but I believe I would have been decent if I'd lived, because I'd have kept close to you. You'll be good to ma— and to Ruth ?"

The sheriff thought that he had drifted away and did not hear the answer, but in a few moments he opened his eyes and said, brightly, " Thank you, Amos." It was the first time that he had used the other man's Christian name.

" Yes, Ned," said the sheriff.

Next morning at daybreak he died. His mother was with him. Just before he went to sleep his mind wandered a little. He fancied that he was a little boy, and that he was sick, and wanted to say his prayers to his mother. " But I'm so sick I can't get out of bed," said he. " God won't mind my saying them in bed, will He ?" Then he folded his hands, and reverently repeated the childish rhyme, and so fell into a peaceful sleep, which deepened into peace. In this wise, perhaps, were answered many prayers.

Amos made all the arrangements the next day. He said that they were going home from Fairport on the day following, but he managed to conclude all the necessary legal formalities in time to take the evening train. Once on the train, and his companions in their sections, he drew a long breath.

" It may not have been Mame that I saw," he
said, taking out his cigar-case on the way to the
smoking-room; "it was merely a glimpse—she
in a buggy, me on foot; and it may be she
wouldn't do a thing or think the game worth
blackmail; but I don't propose to run any
chances in this deal. Hullo — excuse me,
miss!"

The last words were uttered aloud to Ruth
Graves, who had touched him on the arm. He
had a distinct admiration for this young woman, founded on the grounds that she cried very
quietly, that she never was underfoot, and that
she was so unobtrusively kind to Mrs. Smith.

"Anything I can do?" he began, with genuine
willingness.

She motioned him to take a seat. "Mrs.
Smith is safe in her section," she said; "it isn't
that. I wanted to speak to you. Mr. Wickliff,
Ned told me how it was. He said he couldn't
die lying to everybody, and he wanted me to
know how good you were. I am perfectly safe,
Mr. Wickliff," as a look of annoyance puckered
the sheriff's brow. "He told me there was a
woman who might some time try to make money
out of his mother if she could find her, and I was
to watch. Mr. Wickliff, was she rather tall and
slim, with a fine figure?"

"Yes—dark-complected rather, and has a thin face and a largish nose."

"And one of her eyes is a little droopy, and she has a gold filling in her front tooth? Mr. Wickliff, that woman got on this train."

"She did, did she?" said the sheriff, showing no surprise. "Well, my dear young lady, I'm very much obliged to you. I will attend to the matter. Mrs. Smith sha'n't be disturbed."

"Thank you," said the young woman; "that's all. Good-night!"

"You might know that girl had had a business education," the sheriff mused—"says what she's got to say, and moves on. Poor Ned! poor Ned!"

Ruth went to her section, but she did not undress. She sat behind the curtains, peering through the opening at Mrs. Smith's section opposite, or at the lower berth next hers, which was occupied by the sheriff. The curtains were drawn there also, and presently she saw him disappear by sections into their shelter. Then his shoes were pushed partially into the aisle. Empty shoes. She waited; it could not be that he was really going to sleep. But the minutes crept by; a half-hour passed; no sign of life behind his curtains. An hour passed. At the farther end of the car curtains parted, and a

"SHE PAUSED BEFORE MRS. SMITH'S
SECTION"

young woman slipped out of her berth. She
was dark and not handsome, but an elegant
shape and a modish gown made her attrac-
tive-looking. One of her eyelids drooped a
little.

She walked down the aisle and paused before
Mrs. Smith's section, Ruth holding her breath.
She looked at the big shoes on the floor, her lip
curling. Then she took the curtains of Mrs.
Smith's section in both hands and put her head
in.

"I must stop her!" thought Ruth. But she
did not spring out. The sheriff, fully dressed,
was beside the woman, and an arm of iron deliberately turned her round.

"The game's up, Mamie," said Wickliff.

She made no noise, only looked at him.

"What are you going to do?" said she, with
perfect composure.

"Arrest you if you make a racket, talk to you
if you don't. Go into that seat." He indicated
a seat in the rear, and she took it without a
word. He sat near the aisle; she was by the
window.

"I suppose you mean to sit here all night,"
she remarked, scornfully.

"Not at all," said he; "just to the next place.
Then you'll get out."

"Oh, will I ?"

"You will. Either you will get out and go about your business, or you will get out and be taken to jail."

"We're smart. What for ?"

"For inciting prisoners to escape."

"Ned's dead," with a sneer.

"Yes, he's dead, and"—he watched her narrowly, although he seemed absorbed in buttoning his coat—"they say he haunts his old cell, as if he'd lost something. Maybe it's the letter you folded up small enough to go in the seam of a coat. I've got that." He saw that she was watching him in turn, and that she was nervous. "Ned's dead, poor fellow, true enough; but — the girl at Barber & Glasson's ain't dead."

She began to fumble with her gloves, peeling them off and rolling them into balls. He thought to himself that the chances were that she was superstitious.

"Look here," he said, sharply, "have an end of this nonsense ; you get off at the next place, and never bother that old lady again, or—I will have you arrested, and you can try for yourself whether Ned's cell is haunted."

For a brief space they eyed each other, she in an access of impotent rage, he stolid as the carving of the seat. The car shivered; the great wheels moved more slowly. "Decide," said he; not imperatively—dryly, without emotion of any sort. He kept his mild eyes on her.

"It wasn't his mother I meant to tell; it was that girl — that *nice* girl he wanted to marry—"

"You make me tired," said the sheriff. "Are you going, or am I to make a scene and take you? I don't care much."

She slipped her hand behind her into her pocket.

The sheriff laughed, and grasped one wrist.

"*I* don't want to talk to the country fools," she snapped.

"This way," said the sheriff, guiding her. The train had stopped. She laughed as he politely handed her off the platform; the next moment the wheels were turning again and she was gone. He never saw her again.

The porter came out to stand by his side in the vestibule, watching the lights of the station race away and the darkling winter fields fly past. The sheriff was well known to him; he nodded an eager acquiescence to the officer's request: "If those ladies in 8 and 9 ask you any questions, just tell them it was a crazy woman getting the wrong section, and I took care of her."

4

Within the car a desolate mother wept the long night through, yet thanked God amid her tears for her son's last good days, and did not dream of the blacker sorrow that had menaced her and had been hurled aside.

THE CABINET ORGAN

IT was a June day. Not one of those per-
fervid June days that simulate the heat of
July, and try to show the corn what June can
do, but one of Shakespeare's lovely and temperate
days, just warm enough to unfurl the rose petals
of the Armstrong rose-trees and ripen the grass
flowers in the Beaumonts' unmowed yard.

The Beaumonts lived in the north end of town,
at the terminus of the street-car line. They did
not live in the suburbs because they liked space
and country air, nor in order to have flowers and
a kitchen-garden of their own, like the Armstrongs opposite, but because the rent was lower.
The Beaumonts were very poor and very proud.
The Armstrongs were neither poor nor proud.
Joel Armstrong, the head of the family, owned
the comfortable house, with its piazzas and bay-
windows, the small stable and the big yard.
There was a yard enclosed in poultry-netting,

and a pasture for the cow, and the elderly family
horse that had picked up so amazingly under the
influence of good living and kindness that no
one would suspect how cheaply the car company
had sold him.

Armstrong was the foreman of a machine-
shop. Every morning at half-past six Pauline
Beaumont, who rose early, used to see him board
the street car in his foreman's clothes, which
differs from working-men's clothes, though only
in a way visible to the practised observer. He
always was smoking a short pipe, and he usually
was smiling. Mrs. Armstrong was a comely woman, who had a great reputation in the neighborhood as a cook and a nurse. In the family were
three boys—if one can call the oldest a boy, who
was a young carpenter, just this very day setting
up for master-builder. The second boy was fifteen, and in the high - school, and the youngest
was ten. There were no daughters; but for helper
Mrs. Armstrong had a stout young Swede, who
was occasionally seen by the Beaumonts hiding
broken pieces of glass or china in a convenient
ravine. The Beaumont house was much smaller
than the Armstrongs', nor was it in such admirable repair and paint; but then, as Henriette
Beaumont was used to say, " *They* had not a
carpenter in the family."

It will be seen that the Beaumonts held themselves very high above the Armstrongs. They could not forget that twenty-five years ago their father had been Lieutenant-Governor, and they had been accounted rich people in the little Western city. Father and fortune had been lost long since. They were poor, obscure, working hard for a livelihood ; but they still kept their pride, which only increased as their visible consequence diminished. Nevertheless, Pauline often looked wistfully across at the Armstrongs' little feasts and fun, and always walked home on their side of the street. Pauline was the youngest and least proud of the Beaumonts.

To-day, as usual, she came down the street, past the neat low fence of the Armstrongs ; but instead of passing, merely glancing in at the lawn and the house, she stopped ; she leaned her shabby elbows on the gate, where she could easily see the dining-room and sniff the savory odors floating from the kitchen. "Oh, doesn't it smell good ?" she murmured. "Chickens 'fried, and new potatoes, and a strawberry short-cake. They have such a nice garden." She caught her breath in a mirthless laugh. "How absurd I am! I feel like staying here and smelling the whole supper! Yesterday they had waffles, and the day before beefsteak—such lovely, hearty things!"

She was a tall girl, too thin for her height, with a pretty carriage and a delicate irregular face, too colorless and tired for beauty, but not for charm. Her skin was fine and clear, and her brown hair very soft. Her gray eyes were alight with interest as she watched the finishing touches given the table, which was spread with a glossy white cloth, and had a bowl of June roses in the centre. Mrs. Armstrong, in a new dimity gown and white apron, was placing a great platter of golden sponge-cake on the board. She looked up and saw Pauline. The girl could invent no better excuse for her scrutiny (which had such an air of prying) than to drop her head as if in faintness — an excuse, indeed, suggested by her own feelings. In a minute Mrs. Armstrong had stepped through the bay-window and was on the other side of the fence, listening with vivid sympathy to Pauline's shamefaced murmur: "Excuse me, but I feel so ill!"

"It's a rush of blood to the head," cried Mrs. Armstrong, all the instincts of a nurse aroused. "Come right in; you mustn't think of going home. Land! you'll like as not faint before I can get over to you. Hold on to the fence if you feel things swimming!"

Pauline, in her confusion, grew red and redder, while, despite inarticulate protestations, she

"SHE LEANED HER SHABBY ELBOWS ON THE GATE"

was propelled into the house and on to a large lounge.

"Lay your head back," commanded the nurse, appearing with an ammonia-bottle in one hand and a fan in the other.

"It's nothing — nothing at all," gasped Pauline, between shame and the fumes of ammonia. "The day was a little warm, and I walked home, and I was so busy I ate no lunch"—as if that were a change from her habits — "and all at once I felt faint. But I'm all right now."

"Well, I don't *wonder* you're faint," cried Mrs. Armstrong; "you oughtn't to do that way. Now you just got to lie still— Oh, that's only Ikey. Ikey, you get a glass of wine for this lady; it's Miss Beaumont."

The tall young man in the gray suit and the blue flannel shirt blushed a little under his sunburn as he bowed. "Pleased to meet you, miss," said he, promptly, before he disappeared.

"This is a great day for us," continued the mother, releasing the ammonia from duty, and beginning to fan vigorously. "Ike has set up as master-builder—only two men, and he does most of the work; but he's got a house all to himself, and the chance of some bigger ones. We're having a little celebration. You must excuse the paper on the lounge; I put it down when we unpacked the organ."

"Oh, did the organ come?" said the son.

"It surely did, and we've played on it already."

"Why, did you get the music? Was it in the box, too?"

"Oh, we 'ain't played *tunes;* we just have been trying it—like to see how it goes. It's got an awful sweet sound."

"And you ought to hear me play a tune on it, ma."

"You! For the land's sake!"

"Yes, me—that never did play a tune in my life. Anybody can play on that organ." He turned politely to Pauline, as to include her in the conversation. "You see, Miss Beaumont, we're a musical family that can't sing. We can't, as they say, carry a tune to save our immortal souls. The trouble isn't with the voice; it's with our ears. We can hear well enough, too, but we haven't an ear for music. I took lessons once, trying to learn to sing, but the teacher finally braced up to tell me that he hadn't the conscience to take my money. 'What's the matter?' says I. 'You've lots of voice,' says he, 'but you haven't a mite of ear.' 'Can't anybody teach me to sing?' says I. 'Not unless they hypnotize you, like Trilby,' says he. So I gave it up. But next I thought I would learn to play; for if there's one thing ma and the boys and I all love, it's music. And just then, as luck would have it, this teacher wanted to sell his cabinet organ, which is in perfect shape and a fine instrument. And I was craving to buy it, but I knew it was ridiculous, when none of us can play. But I kept thinking. Finally it came to me. I had seen those zither things with numbers on them; why couldn't he paint numbers on the keys of the organ just that way, and make music to correspond? And that's just the way we've done. You're very musical. I—I've often listened to your playing. What do you think of it?" He looked at her wistfully.

"I think it very ingenious—very," said Pauline. She had risen now, and she thanked Mrs. Armstrong, and said she must go home. In truth, she was in a panic at the thought of what she had done. Henriette never would understand. Her heart beat guiltily all the way home.

There were three Beaumonts—Henriette, Mysilla, and Pauline. Henriette and Mysilla were twins, who had dressed alike from childhood's hour, although Mysilla was very plain, a colorless blonde, of small stature and painfully thin, while Henriette was tall, with a stately figure and a handsome dark face that would have looked well on a Roman coin. Yet Henriette was a woman of good taste, and she spent many a night trying to decide on a gown which would suit equally well Mysie's fair head and her glossy black one. Both the black and the brown head were gray now, but they still wore frocks and hats alike. Henriette held that it was the hall-mark of a good family to clothe twins alike, and Henriette did not have her Roman features for nothing. Mysilla had always adored and obeyed Henriette. She gloried in Henriette's haughty beauty and grace, and she was as proud of both now that Henriette was a shabby elderly woman, who had to wear dyed gowns and darned gloves, as in the days when she was the belle of the Iowa capital, and poor Jim Perley fought a duel with Captain Sayre over a misplaced dance on her ball-card. Henriette promised to marry Jim after the duel, but Jim died of pneumonia that very week. For Jim's sake, John Perley, his brother, was good to the girls. Pauline was a baby when her father died. She never remembered the days of pomp, only the lean days of adversity. John Perley obtained a clerkship for her in a music-store.

Henriette gave music lessons. She was a brilliant musician, but she criticised her pupils precisely as she would have done any other equally stupid performers, and her pupils' parents did not always love the truth. Mysilla took in plain sewing, as the phrase goes. She sometimes (since John Perley had given them a sewing-machine) made as much as four dollars a week. They invariably paid their rent in advance, and when they had not money to buy enough to eat they went hungry. They never cared to know their neighbors, and Pauline cringed as she imaged Henriette's sarcasms had she seen her sister drinking the Armstrongs' California port. Henriette had stood in the hall corner and waved Pauline fiercely and silently away while the unconscious Mrs. Armstrong thumped at the broken bell outside, and at last departed, remarking. "Well, they must be gone, or dead!"

Therefore rather timidly Pauline opened the door of the little room that was both parlor and dining-room. Any one could see that the room belonged to people who loved music. The old-fashioned grand-piano was under protection of busts of Bach, Beethoven, and Wagner; and Mysie's violin stood in the corner, near a bookcase full of musical biographies. An air of ex-

quisite neatness was like an aroma of lavender
in the room, and with it was fused a prim good
taste, such as might properly belong to gentlewomen who had learned the household arts
when the rule of three was sacred, and every
large ornament must be attended by a smaller
one on either side. And an observer of a gentle
mind, futhermore, might have found a kind of
pathos in the shabbiness of it all ; for everything fine was worn and faded, and everything
new was coarse. The portrait of the Lieutenant-Governor faced the door. For company it
had on either side small engravings of Webster
and Clay. Beneath it was placed the tea-table,
ready spread. The cloth was of good quality,
but thin with long service. On the table a
large plate of bread held the place of impor-
tance, with two small plates on either corner,
the one containing a tiny slice of suspiciously
yellow butter, and the other a cone of solid
jelly. Such jelly they sell at the groceries out
of firkins. A glass jug of tea stood by a plated
ice-water jug of a pattern highly esteemed before the war. Henriette was stirring a small
lump of ice about the sides of the tea-jug. She
greeted Pauline pleasantly.

"Iced tea?" said Pauline. "I thought we
were to have hot tea and sausages and toast. I

gave Mysie twenty-five cents for them this morning." She did not say that it was the money
for more than one day's luncheon.

"Yes, Mysie said something about it," said
Henriette, "but it didn't seem worth while to
burn up so much wood merely to heat the water
for tea; and toast uses up so much butter."

"But I gave Mysie a dollar to buy a little oil-
stove that we could use in summer; and there
was the sausage; I don't mean to find fault,
sister Etty, but I'm ravenously hungry."

"Of course, child," Henriette agreed, benign-
ly; "you are *always* hungry. But I think you'll
agree I was lucky not to have bought that stove
and those sausages this morning. Who do
you think is coming to this town next week ?
Theodore Thomas, with his own orchestra !
And just as I was going into that store to buy
your stove—though I didn't feel at all sure it
wouldn't explode and burn the house down—
John Perley came up and gave me a ticket, an
orchestra seat; and I said at once, 'The girls
must go too'; but I hadn't but twenty-five cents.
and no more coming in for a week. Then it
occurred to me like a flash, there was this money
you had given me; and, Paula, I made such a
bargain ! The man at Farrell's, where they are
selling the tickets, will get us three seats, not

very far back in the gallery, for my orchestra seat and the money, and we shall have enough money left to take us home in the street cars. Now do you understand ?" concluded Henriette, triumphantly.

"Yes, sister Etty; it will be splendid," responded Pauline, but with less enthusiasm than Henriette had expected.

"Aren't you glad ?" she demanded.

"Oh yes, I'm glad ; but I'm so dead tired I can hardly talk," said Pauline, as she left the room. She felt every stair as she climbed it ; but her face cleared at the sight of Mysie coming through the hall.

"It's a lovely surprise, Mysie, isn't it ?" she cried, cheerfully. She always called Mysie by her Christian name, without prefix. Henriette, although of the same age, was so much more important a person that she would have felt the unadorned name a liberty. But nobody was afraid of Mysie. Pauline wound one of her long arms about her waist and kissed her.

Mysie gave a little gasp of mingled pleasure and relief, and the burden of her thoughts slipped off in the words, "I knew you 'lotted on that oil-stove, Paula, but Etty said you would want me to go—"

"I wouldn't go without you," Pauline burst

in, vehemently, "and I'd live on bread and jelly for a week to give you that pleasure."

"There was the sausage, too; I did feel bad about that; you ought to have good hot meals after working all day."

"No more than you, Mysie."

"I'm not on my feet all day. And I did think of taking some of that seventy-five cents we have saved for the curtains, but I didn't like to spend any without consulting you."

"It's your own money, Mysie; but anyhow I suppose we need the curtains. Go on down; Henriette's calling. I'll be down directly." But after she heard her sister's uncertain foot-step on the stair she stood frowning out of the window at the Armstrong house. "It's hideous to think it," she murmured, "but I don't care— we have so much music and so little sausage! I wish I had the money for my ticket to the concert to spend on meat!"

Then, remorsefully, she went down-stairs, and after supper she played all the evening on the piano; but the airs that she chose were in a simple strain—minstrel songs of a generation ago, like "Nelly was a lady" and "Hard times come again no more," from a battered old book of her mother's.

"Wouldn't you like to try a few Moody and

5

Sankeys ?" Henriette jeered after a while. "Foster seems to me only one degree less maudlin and commonplace. He makes me think of tuberoses !" Pauline laughed and went to the window. The white porcupine of electric light at the corner threw out long spikes of radiance athwart the narrow sidewalk, and a man's shadow dipped into the lighted space. The man was leaning his arms on the fence. "Foolish fellow !" Pauline laughed softly to herself. That night, shortly after she had dropped asleep, she was awakened out of a dream of staying to supper with the Armstrongs, and beholding the board loaded with broiled chickens and plum-pudding, by a clutch on her shoulder. "It was *quite* accidental," she pleaded ; "it really was, sister Etty !" For her dream seemed to project itself into real life, and there was Henriette, a stern figure in flowing white, bending over her.

"Wake up !" she cried. "Listen ! There's something awful happening at the Armstrongs'."

Pauline sat up in bed as suddenly as a jack-in-the-box. Then she gave a little gasp of laughter. "They are all right," said she ; "they are playing on their organ. That's the way they play."

The organ ceased to moan, and Henriette returned to her couch. In ten minutes she was back again, shaking Pauline. "Wake up !" she cried. "How can you sleep in such a racket? He has been murdering popular tunes by inches, and now what he is doing I don't know, but it is *awful*. You know them best. Get up and call to them that we can't sleep for the noise they make."

"I suppose they have a right to play on their own organ."

"They haven't a right to make such a pandemonium anywhere. If you won't do something, I'm going to pretend I think it's cats, and call 'Scat!' and throw something at them."

"You wouldn't hit anything," Pauline returned, in that sleepy tone which always rouses a wakeful sufferer's wrath. "Better shut your window. You can't hear nearly so well then."

"Yes, sister, I'll shut the window," Mysie called from the chamber, as usual eager for peace.

"You let that window alone," commanded Henriette, sternly. A long pause—Henriette seated in rigid agony at the foot of the bed; the Armstrongs experimenting with the Vox Humana stop. "Pauline, do you mean to say that you can sleep? Pauline! *Pauline!*"

"What's the matter now?" asked Pauline.

"I am going to take my brush—no, I shall take *your* brush, Pauline Beaumont—and hurl it at them!"

"Oh, sister, please don't," begged Mysie from within, like the voices on a stage.

Henriette spoke not again; she strode out of the room, and did even as she had threatened. She flung Pauline's brush straight at the organist sitting before the window. Whether she really meant to injure young Armstrong's candid brow is an open question; and, judging from the result, I infer that she did not mean to do more than scare her sister; therefore she aimed afar. By consequence the missile sped straight into the centre of the window. But not through it; the window was raised, and a wire screen rattled the brush back with a shivering jar.

"What's that? A bat?" said Armstrong, happily playing on. His father and mother were beaming upon him in deep content—his father a trifle sleepy, but resolved, the morrow being Sunday, to enjoy this musical hour to the full, his mother seated beside him and reading the numbers aloud.

"You see, Ikey," she had explained, "that's what makes you slow. While you're reading the numbers, you lose 'em on the organ; and while you're finding the numbers on the keys, you loose 'em on the paper. I'll read them awful low, so no one would suspect, and you keep your whole mind on those keys. Now begin again ; I've got a pin to prick them—2-4-3, 1-3—no, 1-8. 1-8—it's only one 1-8: guess we better begin again."

So Mrs. Armstrong droned forth the numbers and Ikey hammered them on the organ, pumping with his feet, whenever he did not forget. The two boys slept peacefully through the weird clamor. The neighbors, with one exception, were apparently undisturbed. That exception, named Henriette Beaumont, heard with swelling wrath.

"I've thrown the brush," said she. No response from the pillow. "Now I'm going to throw the broken - handled mug," continued Henriette, in a tone of deadly resolve; "it's heavy, and it may kill some one, but I can't help it!" Still a dead silence. *Crash! smash!* The mug with the broken handle had sped against the weather-boarding.

"Now what was *that?*" cried Ike, jumping up. Before he was on his feet a broken soap-dish had followed the mug. Up flew the sash, and Ike was out of the window. "What are you doing that for? What do you mean by that?" he yelled, to which the dark and silent house opposite naturally made no reply. Ike was out in the road now, and both his parents were after him. The elder Armstrong had been so suddenly wakened from a doze that he was under the impression of a fire somewhere, and let out a noble shout to that effect. Mrs. Armstrong, convinced that a dynamite bomb had missed fire, gathered her skirts tightly around her ankles—as if bombs could run under them like mice—and helped by screaming alternately "Police!" and "Murder!"

Henriette gloated silently over the confusion. It did her soul good to see Ike Armstrong running along the sidewalk after supposititious boys.

The Armstrongs did not return to the organ. Henriette heard their footsteps on the gravel, she heard the muffled sound of voices; but not again did the tortured instrument excite her nerves, and she sank into a troubled slumber. As they sat at breakfast the next morning, and Henriette was calculating the share due each cup from the half-pint of boiled milk, the broken bell-wire jangled. Pauline said she would go.

"It can't be any one to call so early in the morning," said Henriette; "you may go."

It was young Armstrong, in his Sunday clothes. Pauline's only picture of him had been in his work-a-day garb; it was curious how differently he impressed her, fresh from the bath and the razor, trigly buttoned up in a perfectly fitting suit of blue and brown, with a dazzling rim of

"'SOMEBODY THREW THESE THINGS AT OUR WINDOW'"

white against his shapely tanned throat, and a crimson rose in his button-hole. "How handsome he is!" thought Pauline. She had never been satisfied with her own nose, and she looked at the straight bridge of his and admired it. She was too innocent and ignorant herself to notice how innocently clear were his eyes: but she thought that they looked true and kind, and she did notice the bold lines of his chin and jaw, and the firm mouth under his black mustache. Unaccountably she grew embarrassed: he was looking at her so gravely, almost sternly, his new straw hat in one hand, and the other slightly extended to her and holding a neat bundle.

He bowed ceremoniously, as he had seen actors bow on the stage. "Somebody threw these things at our window last night," said he; "I think they belong to you. I couldn't find all the pieces of the china."

"They weren't all there," stammered Pauline, foolishly; and then a wave of mingled confusion and irritation at her false position — there was her monogram on the ivory brush!—and a queer kind of amusement, swept over her, and dyed her delicate cheek as red as Armstrong's rose. And suddenly he, too, flushed, and his eyes flashed.

"I'm sorry I disturbed your sister," said he, "but I hope she will not throw any more things

at us.   We will try not to practise so late another
night.   Good-morning."

"I *am* sorry," said Pauline ; "tell your mother I'm sorry, please.   She was so kind to me."

"Thank you," Armstrong said, heartily ; "I
will."   And somehow before he went they shook
hands.

Pauline gave the message, but she felt so
guilty because of this last courtesy that she gave
it without reproach, even though her only good
brush disclosed a pitiful crack.

"Well, you know why I did it," said Henriette, coolly ; "and does the man suppose his
playing isn't obnoxious any hour of the day as
well as night?   But let us hope they will be
quiet awhile.   Paula, have you any money?   We
ought to go over those numbers for the concert
beforehand, and we must get Verdi's Requiem.
Mysie has some, but she wants it to buy curtains."

"I'm sorry, sister Etty, but I haven't a cent."

"Then the curtains will have to wait, Mysie,"
said Henriette, cheerfully, "for we must have
the music to-morrow."

Mysie threw a deprecating glance at Pauline.
"There was a bargain in chintzes," she began,
feebly, "but of course, sister, if Paula doesn't
mind—"

"I don't mind, Mysie," said Pauline.

Why should she make Mysie unhappy and
Henriette cross for a pair of cheap curtains?
The day was beautiful, and she attended church.
She was surprised, looking round at the choir,
to discover young Armstrong in the seat behind
her. She did not know that he attended that
church. But surely there was no harm in a
neighbor's walking home with Mysie and her.
How well and modestly he talked, and how gentle and deferential he was to Mysie! Mysie
sighed when he parted from them, a little way
from the house.

"That young man is very superior to his station," she declared, solemnly; "he must be of
good though decayed family."

"His grandfather was a Vermont farmer, and
ours was a Massachusetts farmer," retorted Pauline; "I dare say if we go back far enough we
shall find the Armstrongs as good as we—"

"Oh, pray don't talk that way before Etty,
dear," interrupted Mysie, hurriedly: "she thinks
it so like the anarchists: and if you get into that
way of speech, you *might* slip out something before her. Poor Etty, I wish she felt as if she
could go to church. I hope she had a peaceful
morning."

Ah, hope unfounded! Never had Miss Hen-

riette Beaumont passed a season more rasping to
her nerves. Looking out of the window, she
saw both the younger Armstrongs and their mother. The boys had been picking vegetables.

"Now, boys," called Mrs. Armstrong, gayly,
"let's come and play on the organ."

Henriette's soul was in arms. Unfortunately
she was still in the robes of rest (attempting to
slumber after her tumultuous night), and dignity forbade her shouting out of the window.

The two boys passed a happy morning experimenting on the different stops, and improvising
melodies of their own. "Say, mummy, isn't
that kinder like a *tune?*" one or the other would
exclaim. Mrs. Armstrong listened with pride.
The awful combination of discords fell sweetly
on her ear, which was "no ear for music."

"It's just lovely to have an organ," she thought.

When Miss Beaumont could bear no more she
attired herself and descended the stairs. Then
the boys stopped. In the afternoon several
friends of the Armstrongs called. They sang
Moody and Sankey hymns, until Henriette was
pale with misery.

"I think I prefer the untutored Armstrong
savages themselves, with their war-cries," she
remarked.

"Perhaps they will get tired of it," Mysie prof-

"'NOW, BOYS, LET'S COME AND PLAY ON THE ORGAN'"

fered for consolation. But they did not tire. They never·played later than nine o'clock at night again, but until that hour the music-loving and unmusical family played and sang to their hearts' content. And the Beaumonts saw them at the Thomas concert, Ike and his mother and Jim, applauding everything. Henriette said the sight made her ill.

Time did not soften her rancor. She caught cold at the concert, and for two weeks was confined to her chamber with what Mrs. Armstrong called rheumatism, but Henriette called gout. During the time she assured Mysie that what she suffered from the Armstrong organ exceeded anything that gout could inflict.

"Do let me speak to Mrs. Armstrong," begged Mysie.

"I spoke to that boy, the one with the freckles, myself yesterday," replied Henriette, "out of the window. I told him if they didn't stop I would have them indicted."

"Why, how did you see him?" Mysie was aghast, but she dared not criticise Henriette.

"He came here with a bucket of water. Said his mother saw us taking water out of the well, and it was dangerous. The impertinent woman, she actually offered to send us water from their cistern every day."

"But I think that was — was rather kind, sister, and it would be dreadful to have typhoid fever."

"I would rather *die* of typhoid fever than have that woman bragging to her vulgar friends that she gives the Beaumonts, Governor Beaumont's daughters, *water!* I know what her *kindness* means." Thus Henriette crushed Mysie. But when the organ began, and it was evident that Tim Armstrong intended to learn "Two Little Girls in Blue," if it took him all the afternoon, Mysie rose.

"Mysie," called Henriette, "don't you go one step to the Armstrongs'."

Mysie sat down, but in a little while she tried again.

"I wish you'd let Paula, then; she is going by there every day, and she has had no dispute with them. She often stops to talk."

"Talk to whom?" said Henriette, icily.

"Oh, to any of them — Tim or Pete or Mrs. Armstrong."

"Does she talk to them long?"

"Oh no, not very long — just as she goes by. I think you're mistaken, sister. They don't think such mean things. Truly they are—nice; they seem very fond of each other, and they almost always give Paula flowers."

" What does she do with the flowers ?"

" She puts them in the vases, and wears them."

" Do they give her anything else ?" Henriette's tone was so awful that Mysie dropped her work.

" Do they ?" persisted Henriette.

" They sent over the magazines a few times, but that was just borrowing, and once they— they — sent over some shortcake and some — bread."

Henriette sat bolt-upright in bed, reckless of the pain every movement gave her.

" Mysilla Beaumont, do you see where your sister is drifting ? Are you both crazy ? But I shall put a stop to this nonsense this very day. I am going to write a note to John Perley, and you will have to take it. Bring me the paper. If there isn't any in my desk, take some out of Pauline's."

" Oh, Henriette," whimpered Mysie, " *what* are you going to do ?"

" You will soon see, and you will have to help me. After they have been disgraced and laughed at, we'll see whether she will care to lean over their fence and talk to them."

It was true that Pauline did talk to the Armstrongs ; she did lean over the Armstrong fence. It had come to pass by degrees. She knew per-

fectly well it was wrong. Henriette never al-
lowed her to have any acquaintances. But Henriette could not see her from the bed, and Mysie
did not mind; and so she fell into the habit
of stopping at the Armstrong gate to inquire
for Mrs. Armstrong's turkeys, or to ask advice
about the forlorn little geraniums which fought
for life in the Beaumont yard, or to lend her
own nimble fingers to the adorning of Mrs. Armstrong's bonnets. She saw Ike often. Once she
actually ventured to enter "those mechanics'"
doors and play on the detested organ. Her musical gifts could not be compared to her sister's.
A sweet, true voice, of no great compass, a touch
that had only sympathy and a moderate facility
—these the highly cultivated Beaumonts rated
at their very low artistic value; but the ignorant
Armstrongs listened to Pauline's hymns in rapt-
ure. The tears filled Mrs. Armstrong's eyes:
impulsively she kissed the girl. "Oh, you dear
child!" she cried. Ike said nothing. Not a
word. He was standing near enough to Pauline
to touch the folds of her dress. His fingers almost reverently stroked the faded pink muslin.
He swallowed something that was choking him.
Joel Armstrong nodded and smiled. Then his
eyes sought his wife's. He put out his hand and
held hers. When the music was done and the

young people were gone, he puffed hard on his dead pipe, saying, "It's the best thing that can happen to a young man, mother, to fall in love with a real good girl, ain't it?"

"Yes, I guess it is."

"And I guess you'd have the training of this one, mother; and there's plenty of room in the lot opposite that's for sale to build a nice little house. They'd start a sight better off than we did."

"But we were very happy. Joe, weren't we?"

"That we were, and that we are, Sally," said Armstrong. "Come on out in the garden with your beau: we ain't going to let the young folks do all the courting."

Mysie and Henriette saw the couple walking in the garden, the husband's arm around his wife's waist, and the soft-hearted sister sighed.

"Oh, sister, don't you kinder wish you *hadn't done it?*" she whispered. "They didn't mean any harm."

"Harm? No. I dare say that young carpenter would be willing to marry Pauline Beaumont!" cried Henriette, bitterly.

Mysie shook her gray head, her loose mouth working, while she winked away a tear. "I don't care, I don't care"— thus did she inwardly

moan out a spasm of dire resolution—" I'm just
going to tell Pauline !''

Perhaps what she told set the cloud on the
girl's pretty face ; and perhaps that was why she
looked eagerly over the Armstrong fence every
night ; and the cloud lifted at the sound of Mrs.
Armstrong's mellow voice hailing her from any
part of the house or yard.

But one night, instead of the usual cheerful
stir about the house, she found the Swede girl
alone in the kitchen, weeping over the potatoes.
To Pauline's inquiries she returned a burst of
woe. " 'They all tooken to chail—all !" she
wailed. " I don't know what to do if I get supper. The mans come, the police mans, and
tooken them all away. *I hela verlden!* who ever
know such a country ? Such nice peoples sent
to chail for play on the organ—their own organ !
They say they not play right, but I think to send
to chail for not play right on the organ that
sha'n't be right !"

Pauline could make nothing more out of her;
but the man on the corner looked in at one particularly dolorous burst of sobs over poor Tim
and poor Petey and tendered his version :
" They've gone, sure enough, miss. Your sisters have had them arrested for keeping and
committing a nuisance. Now, I ain't stuck on

their organ-playing, as a general rule. myself. but I wouldn't go so far as to call it a nuisance. But the Fullers ain't on the best of terms ; old Fuller is a crank, and there's politics between him and Armstrong and the Delaneys, who have just moved into the neighborhood, mother and daughter — very musical folks, they say, and nervous ; they have joined in with your sister—"

"Where have they gone ?" asked Pauline, who was very pale.

"To the police court. They were mighty cunning, if you'll excuse me, miss. They picked out that old German crank, Von Reibnitz, who plays in the Schubert Quartet, and loves music better than beer."

The man was right. Henriette had chosen her lawgiver shrewdly. At this very moment she was sitting in one of the dingy chairs of the police court, with the mien of Marie Antoinette on her way to execution. Mysie sat beside her in misery not to be described ; for was she not joined with Henriette in the prosecution of the unfortunate Armstrongs? and had she not surreptitiously partaken of hot rolls and strawberry jam that very day, handed over the fence to her by Mrs. Armstrong ? She could not sustain the occasional glare of the magistrate's glasses ; and, unable to look in the direction of the betrayed

6

Armstrongs, for the most part she peered deso-
lately at the clerk. The accused sat opposite.
Mr. Armstrong and Ike were in their working-
clothes. Hastily summoned, they had not the
meagre comfort of a toilet. The father looked
about the court, a perplexed frown replacing at
intervals a perplexed grin. When he was not
studying the court-room, he was polishing the
bald spot on his head with a large red handkerchief, or rubbing the grimy palms of his hands
on the sides of his trousers. He had insisted
upon an immediate trial, but his wits had not
yet pulled themselves out of the shock of his arrest. The boys varied the indignant solemnity
of bearing which their mother had impressed on
them with the unquenchable interest of their
age. Mrs. Armstrong had assumed her best bonnet and her second-best gown. She was a handsome woman, with her fair skin, her wavy brown
hair, and brilliant blue eyes; and the reporter
looked at her often, adding to the shame and
fright that were clawing her under her Spartan
composure. But she held her head in the air
bravely. Not so her son, who sat with his hands
loosely clasped before him and his head sunk on
his breast through the entire arraignment.

Behind the desk the portly form of the magistrate filled an arm-chair to overflowing, so that

the reporter wondered whether he could rise from
the chair, should it be necessary, or whether chair
and he must perforce cling together. His body
and arms were long, but his legs were short, so
he always used a cricket, which somehow de-
tracted from the dignity of his appearance. He
had been a soldier, and kept a martial gray mustache ; but he wore a wig of lustrous brown
locks, which he would push from side to side in
the excitement of a case, and then clap frankly
back into place with both hands. There was no
deceit about Fritz Von Reibnitz. He was a man
of fiery prejudices, but of good heart and sound
sense, and he often was shrewder than the lawyers who tried to lead him through his weak-
nesses. But he had a leaning towards a kind of
free-hand, Arabian justice, and rather followed
the spirit of the law than servilely questioned
what might be the letter. Twirling his mus-
tachios, he leaned back in his chair and studied
the faces of the Armstrong family, while the
clerk read the information slowly—for the ben-
efit of his friend the reporter, who felt this to
be one of the occasions that enliven a dusty road
of life.

"State of Iowa, Winfield County. The City
of Fairport vs. Jos. L. Armstrong, Mrs. J. L.
Armstrong, Isaac J. Armstrong, Peter Arm-

strong, and Timothy Armstrong. The defendants" (the names were repeated, and at each
name the mother of the Armstrongs winced)
"are accused of the crime of violating Section 2
of Chapter 41 of the ordinances of said city.
For that the defendants, on the 3d, the 10th,
the 15th, and 23d day of July, 18—, in the city
of Fairport, in said county, did conspire and
confederate together to disturb the public quiet
of the neighborhood, and in pursuance of said
conspiracy, and aiding and abetting each other,
did make, then and there, loud and unusual
noises by playing on a cabinet organ in an unusual and improper manner, and by singing
boisterously and out of tune ; and did thereby
disturb the public quiet of the neighborhood.
contrary to the ordinances in such case pro-
vided."

"You vill read also the ordinance, Mr. Clerk,"
called the magistrate, with much majesty of manner, frowning at the same time on the younger
lawyers, who were unable to repress their feelings, while the reporter appeared to be taken
with cramps.

The clerk read :

"Every person who shall unlawfully disturb
the public quiet of any street, alley, avenue, public square, wharf, or any religious or other public

assembly, or building public or private, or any neighborhood, private family, or person within the city, by giving false alarms of fire " (Mrs. Armstrong audibly whispered to her husband, " We *never* did that !"). " by loud or unusual noises " (Mrs. Armstrong sank back in her corner, and Joseph Armstrong very nearly groaned aloud), " by ringing bells, blowing horns or other instruments, etc., etc., shall be deemed guilty of a misdemeanor, and punished accordingly."

Then up rose the attorney for the prosecution to state his case. He narrated how the Armstrong family had bought an organ, and had played upon it almost continually since the purchase, thereby greatly annoying and disturbing the entire neighborhood. He said that no member of the Armstrong family knew more than two changes on the organ, and that several of them, in addition to playing, were accustomed to sing in a loud and disagreeable voice (the Armstrong family were visibly affected), and that so great was the noise and disturbance made by the said organ that the prosecuting witness, Miss Beaumont, who was sick at the time. had been agitated and disturbed by it, to her great bodily and mental damage and danger. That although requested to desist, they had not desisted (Tim and Pete exchanged glances of undissembled enjoyment), and therefore she was compelled in self-defence to invoke the aid of the law.

Ike listened dully. There was no humor in the situation for him. He felt himself and his whole family disgraced, dragged before the police magistrate just like a common drunk and disorderly loafer, and accused of being a nuisance to their neighborhood ; the shame of it tingled to his finger - tips. He would not look up; it seemed to him that he could never hold up his head again. No doubt it would all be in the paper next morning, and the Armstrongs, who were so proud of their honest name, would be the laughing-stock of the town. Somebody was saying something about a lawyer. Ike scowled at the faces of the young attorneys lolling and joking outside the railing. "I won't fool away any money on those chumps," he growled ; "I want to get through and pay my fine and be done."

Somebody laughed ; then he saw that it was the sheriff of the county, a good friend of his. He looked appealingly up at the strong, dark face ; he grasped the big hand extended.

"I'm in a hole, Mr. Wickliff," he whispered.

"Naw, you're not," replied Wickliff ; "you've a friend in the family. She got onto this plot and came to me a good while ago. We're all ready. I've known her since she was a little girl. Know 'em all, poor things! Say, let *me* act as your attorney. Don't have to be a member of the bar to practise in *this* court. Y'Honor! If it please y'Honor, I'd like to be excused to telephone to some witnesses for the defence."

Ike caught his breath. "A friend in the family!" He did not dare to think what that meant. And Wickliff had gone. They were examining the prosecuting witnesses. Miss Mysilla Beaumont took the oath, plainly frightened. She spoke almost in a whisper. Her evident desire to deal gently with the Armstrongs was used skilfully by the young attorney whom John Perley (his uncle) had employed. Behold (he made poor Mysie's evidence seem to say) what ear-rending and nerve-shattering sounds these barbarous organists must have produced to make this amiable lady protest at law! Mysie fluttered out of the witness-box in a tremor, nor dared to look where Mrs. Armstrong sat bridling and fanning herself. Next three Fullers deposed to more or less disturbance from the musical taste of the Armstrongs, and the Delaney daughter swore, in a clarion voice, that the playing of the Armstrongs was the worst ever known.

"It ain't any worse than her scales!" cried

Mrs. Armstrong, goaded into speech. The magistrate darted a warning glance at her.

Miss Henriette Beaumont was called last. Her mourning garments, to masculine eyes, did not show their age ; and her grand manner and handsome face, with its gray hair and its flashing eyes, caused even the magistrate's manner to change. Henriette had a rich voice and a beautiful articulation. Every softly spoken word reached Mrs. Armstrong, who writhed in her seat. She recited how she had spent hours of "absolute torment" under the Armstrong instrumentation, and she described in the language of the musician the unspeakable iniquities of the Armstrong technique. Her own lawyer could not understand her, but the magistrate nodded in sympathy. She said she was unable to sleep nights because of the " horrible discords played on the organ—"

" I declare we never played it but two nights, and they weren't discords ; they were nice tunes," sobbed Mrs. Armstrong.

The justice rapped and frowned. " Silence in der court !" he thundered. Then he glared on poor Mrs. Armstrong. " Anybody vot calls hisself a laty ought to behave itself like sooch !" he said, with strong emphasis. The attorneys present choked and coughed. In fact, the remark passed into a saying in police-court circles. Miss Henriette stepped with stately graciousness to her seat.

"Und now der defence." said the justice— "der Armstrong family. Vot has you got to say?"

"Let me put some witnesses on first, Judge," called Wickliff. "to show the Armstrongs' character." He was opening the door, and the hall behind seemed filled.

"Oh, good land. Ikey. do look!" quavered Mrs. Armstrong; "there's pa's boss, and the Martins that used to live in the same block with us, and Mrs. O'Toole, and all the neighbors most up to the East End, and—oh, Ikey! there's Miss Pauline herself! Our friends 'ain't deserted us; I knew perfectly well they *wouldn't!*"

Ike did look up then—he stood up. His eyes met the eyes of his sweetheart, and he sat down with his cheeks afire and his head in the air.

"In the first place," said Wickliff, assuming an easy attitude, with one hand in a pocket and the other free for oratorical display, "I'll call Miss Beaumont, Miss Henriette Beaumont, for the defence." Miss Beaumont responded to the call, and turned a defiant stare on the amateur attorney.

"You say you were disturbed by the Armstrongs' organ?"

"I was painfully disturbed."

"Naturally you informed your neighbors, and asked them to desist playing the organ?"

"I did."

"How many times?"

"Once."

"To whom did you speak?"

"I told the boys to tell their mother."

"Are you passionately fond of music?"

"I am."

"Are you sensitive to bad music—acutely sensitive?"

"I suppose I am; a lover of music is, of necessity."

The magistrate nodded and sighed.

"Are you of a particularly patient and forbearing disposition?" Henriette directed a withering glance at the tall figure of the questioner.

"I am forbearing enough," she answered. "Do I need to answer questions that are plainly put to insult me?"

"No, madam," said the magistrate. "Mr. Wickliff, I rules dot question out."

Nothing daunted, Wickliff continued: "When you gave the boys warning, where were they?"

" In my house."

" How came they there ?"

"They had brought over a bucket of water."

" Why ?"

" Because we had only well-water, they said."

" That was rather kind on the part of Mrs. Armstrong, don't you think ? In every respect, besides playing the organ, she was a kind neighbor, wasn't she ?"

" I don't complain of her."

" Wasn't she rather noted in the neighborhood as a lady of great kindness ? Didn't she often send in little delicacies—flowers, fruit, and such things—gifts that often pass between neighbors to different people ?"

" She may have. I am not acquainted with her."

" Hasn't she sent in things at different times to *you* ?"

Henriette's throat began to form the word no: then she remembered the shortcake, she remembered the roses, she remembered her oath, and she choked. " I don't know much about it ; perhaps she may have," said she.

" That will do," said Wickliff. " Call Miss Mysilla Beaumont." Wickliff's respectful bearing reassured the agitated spinster. He wouldn't detain her a moment. He only wanted to know had neighborly courtesies passed between the two houses. Yes? Had Mrs. Armstrong been a kind and unobtrusive neighbor?

"Oh yes, sir; yes, indeed," cried poor Mysie.

"Were you yourself much disturbed by the organ?"

"No, sir," gasped Mysie, with one tragic glance at her sister's stony features. She knew now what Jeanie Deans must have suffered.

"That will do," said Wickliff.

Then a procession of witnesses filed into the narrow space before the railing. First the employer of the elder Armstrong gave his high praise of his foreman as a man and a citizen; then came the neighbors, declaring the Armstrong virtues—from Mrs. Martin, who deposed with tears that Mrs. Armstrong's courage and good nursing had saved her little Willy's life when he was burned, to Mrs. O'Toole, an aged little Irish woman, who recited how the brave young Peter had rescued her dog from a band of young torturers. "And they had a tin can filled with fire-crackers, yer Honor (an' they was lighted), tied to the poor stoompy tail of him; but Petey he pulled it aff, and he throwed it ferninst them, and he made them sorry that day, he did, for it bursted. He's a foine bye, and belongs to a foine family!"

"Aren't you a little prejudiced in favor of the Armstrongs, Mrs. O'Toole?" asked the prosecuting attorney, as Wickliff smilingly bade him "take the witness."

"Yes, sor, I am," cried Mrs. O'Toole, huddling her shawl closer about her wiry little frame. "I am that, sor, praise God! They paid the rint for me whin me bye was in throuble, and they got him wur-rk, and he's doin' well this day, and been for three year. And there's many a hot bite passed betwane us whin we was neighbors. Prejudecced! I'd not be wuth the crow's pickin's if I wasn't; and the back of me hand and the sowl of me fut to thim that's persecuting of thim this day!"

"Call Miss Pauline Beaumont," said Wickliff. "That will do, grandma."

Pauline's evidence was very concise, but to the point. She did not consider the Armstrong organ a nuisance. She believed the Armstrongs, if instructed, would learn to play the organ. If the window were shut the noise could not disturb any one. She had the highest respect and regard for the Armstrongs.

"There's my case, your Honor," said Wickliff, "and I've confidence enough in it and in this court to leave it in your hands. Say the same, Johnny?"—to the young lawyer. Perley laughed;

he was beginning to suspect that not all the case appeared on the surface. Perhaps the Beaumont family peace would fare all the better if he kept his hands off. He said that he had no evidence to offer in rebuttal, and would leave the case confidently to the wisdom of the court.

"And I'll bet you a hat on one thing, Amos," he observed in an undertone to the amateur attorney on the other side, " Fritz's decision on this case may be good sense, but it will be awful queer law."

" Fritz has got good sense," said Amos.

The magistrate announced his decision. He had deep sympathy, he said, for the complainant, a gifted and estimable lady. He knew that the musical temperament was sensitive as the violin —yes. But it also appeared from the evidence that the Armstrong family were a good, a worthy family, lacking only a knowledge of music to make them acceptable neighbors. Therefore he decided that the Armstrong family should hire a competent teacher, and that, until able to play without giving offence to the neighbors, they should close the window. With that understanding he would find the defendants not guilty ; and each party must pay its own costs.

Perley glanced at Amos, who grinned and repeated, "Fritz has got good sense."

"'THEY HAVE ENGAGED ME'"

"I'd have won my hat," said Perley, "but I'm not kicking. Just look at Miss Beaumont, though."

Henriette had listened in stony calm. She did not once look at Pauline, who was standing at the other side of the room. "Come, sister," she said to Mysie. Mysie turned a scared face on Henriette. She drew her aside.

"Did you hear what he said?" she whispered. "Oh, Henriette, *what* shall we do? We shall have to pay the costs—"

"The Armstrongs will have to pay them too," said Henriette, grimly.

"Theirs won't be so much, because none of their witnesses will take a cent; but the Fullers and Miss Delancy want their fees, and it's a dollar and a half, and there's—"

"We shall have to borrow it from John Perley," said Henriette.

"But he isn't here, and maybe they'll put us in jail if we don't pay. Oh, Henriette, why did you—"

This, Mysie's first and last reproach of her sovereign, was cut short by the approach of Pauline.

At her side walked young Armstrong. And Pauline, who used to be so timid, presented him without a tremor.

"I wanted to tell you, Miss Beaumont," said Ike, "that I did not understand that we were disturbing you so much when you were sick. Not being musical, we could not appreciate what we were making you suffer. But I beg you to believe, ma'am, that we are all very sorry. And I didn't think it no more than right that I should pay all the costs of this case—which I have done gladly. I hope you will forgive us, and that we may all of us live as good neighbors in future. We will try not to annoy you, and we have engaged a very fine music-teacher."

"They have engaged *me*," said Pauline. And as she spoke she let the young man very gently draw her hand into his arm.

HIS DUTY

.

AMOS WICKLIFF little suspected himself riding, that sunny afternoon, towards the ghastliest adventure of an adventurous life. Nevertheless, he was ill at ease. His horse was too light for his big muscles and his six feet two of bone. Being a merciful man to beasts, he could not ride beyond a jog-trot, and his soul was fretted by the delay. He cast a scowl down the dejected neck of the pony to its mournful, mismated ears, and from thence back at his own long legs, which nearly scraped the ground. "O Lord! ain't I a mark on this horse!" he groaned. "We could make money in a circus!" With a gurgle of disgust he looked about him at the glaring blue sky, at the measureless, melancholy sweep of purple and dun prairie.

"Well, give *me* Iowa!" said Amos.

For a long while he rode in silence, but

his thoughts were distinct enough for words.
"What an amusing little scamp it was!"—thus
they ran—"I believe he could mimic anything
on earth. He used to give a cat and puppy
fighting that I laughed myself nearly into a fit
over. When I think of that I hate this job.
Now why? You never saw the fellow to speak
to him more than twice. Duty, Amos, duty.
But if he is as decent as he's got the name of being here, it's rough— Hullo! River? Trees?"
The river might be no more than the lightening
rim of the horizon behind the foliage, but there
was no mistake about the trees ; and when Wickliff turned the field-glass, which he habitually
carried, on them he could make out not only the
river and the willows, but the walls of a cabin
and the lovely undulations of a green field of
corn. Half an hour's riding brought him to the
house and a humble little garden of sweet-pease
and hollyhocks. Amos groaned. "How cursed
decent it all looks! And flowers too! I have
no doubt that his wife's a nice woman, and the
baby has a clean face. Everything certainly
does combine to ball me up on this job! There
she is ; and she's nice!"

A woman in a clean print gown, with a child
pulling at her skirt, had run to the gate. She
looked young. Her freckled face was not ex-

actly pretty, but there was something engaging in the flash of her white teeth and her soft, black-lashed, dark eyes. She held the gate wide open, with the hospitality of the West. "Won't you 'light, stranger?" she called.

, "I'm bound for here." replied Amos, telling his prepared tale glibly. "This is Mr. Brown's. the photographer's, ain't it? I want him to come to the settlement with me and take me standing on a deer."

"Yes, sir." The woman spoke in mellow Southern accents, and she began to look inter-ested. as suspecting a romance under this vain-glory. "Yes, sir. Deer you shot. I reckon. I'll send Johnny D. for him. Oh, Johnny D. !"

A lath of a boy of ten, with sunburnt white hair and bright eyes, vaulted over a fence and ran to her, receiving her directions to go find uncle after he had cared for the gentleman's horse.

"Your nephew, madam?" said Amos. as the lad's bare soles twinkled in the air.

"Well, no, sir, not born nephew." she said, smiling ; "he's a little neighbor boy. His folks live three miles further down the river ; but I reckon we all think jest as much of him as if he was our born kin. Won't you come in, sir ?"

By this time she had passed under the luxuriant arbor of honeysuckle that shaded the porch, and she threw wide the door. The room was large. It was very tidy. The furniture was of the sort that can be easily transported where railways have to be pieced out with mule trails. But it was hardly the ordinary pioneer cabin. Not because there was a sewing-machine in one corner, for the sewing-machine follows hard on the heels of the plough ; perhaps because of the white curtains at the two windows (curtains darned and worn thin by washing, tied back with ribbons faded by the same ministry of neatness), or the square of pretty though cheap carpet on the floor, or the magazines and the bunch of sweet-pease on the table, but most because of the multitude of photographs on the clumsy walls. They were on cards, all of the same size (not more than 8 by 10 inches), protected by glass, and framed in mossy twigs. Some of the pictures were scenes of the country, many of them bits of landscape near the house, all chosen with a marvellous elimination of the usual grotesque freaks of the camera, and with such an unerring eye for subject and for light and shade that the artist's visions of the flat, commonplace country were not only picturesque but poetic. In the prints also were an extraordinary richness and range of tone. It did not seem possible that

mere black and white could give such an effect
of brilliancy and depth of color. An artist looking over this obscure photographer's workman-
ship might feel a thrill like that which crinkles
a flower-lover's nerves when he sees a mass of
azaleas in fresh bloom.

Amos was not an artist, but he had a camera at
home, and he gave a gulp of admiration. " Well,
he *is* great!" he sighed. " That beats any photographic work I ever saw."

The wife's eyes were luminous. " Ain't he!"
said she. " It 'most seems wicked for him to be
farming when he can do things like that—"

" Why does he farm ?"

" It's his health. He caynt stand the climate
East."

" You are from the South yourself, I take it ?"

" Yes, sir, Arkansas, though I don't see how
ever you guessed it. I met Mist' Brown there,
down in old Lawrence. I was teaching school
then, and went to have my picture taken in his
wagon. Went with my father, and he was so
pleasant and polite to paw I liked him from the
start. He nursed paw during his last sickness.
Then we were married and came out here—
You're looking at that piture of little Davy at
the well ? I like that the best of all the ten; his
little dress looks so cute, and he has such a sweet

smile; and it's the only one has his hair smooth.
I tell Mist' Brown I do believe he musses that
child's hair himself—"

"Papa make Baby's hair pitty for picture!"
cried the child, delighted to have understood
some of the conversation.

"He's a very pretty boy," said Amos. "'Fraid
to come to me, young feller?"

But the child saw too few to be shy, and happily perched himself on the tall man's shoulder,
while he studied the pictures. The mother appeared as often as the child.

"He's got her at the best every time," mused
the observer; "best side of her face, best light
on her nose. Never misses. That's the way a
man looks at his girl; always twists his eyes a
little so as to get the best view. Plainly she's in
love with him, and looks remarkably like he was
in love with her, damn him!" Then, with great
civility, he asked Mrs. Brown what developer her
husband used, and listened attentively, while she
showed him the tiny dark room leading out of
the apartment, and exhibited the meagre stock
of drugs.

"I keep them up high and locked up in that
cupboard with the key on top, for fear Baby
might git at them," she explained. She evi-
dently thought them a rare and creditable col-

lection. "I ain't a bit afraid of Johnny D.; he's sensible. and, besides, he minds every word Mist' Brown tells him. He sets the world by Mist' Brown : always has ever since the day Mist' Brown saved him from drowning in the eddy."

"How was that?"

"Why, you see, he was out fishing, and climbed out on a log and slipped someway. It's about two miles further down the river, between his parents' farm and ours; and by a God's mercy we were riding by, Dave and the baby and I— the baby wasn't out of long-clothes then—and we heard the scream. Dave jumped out and ran. peeling his clothes as he ran. I only waited to throw the weight out of the wagon to hold the horses. and ran after him. I could see him plain in the water. Oh, it surely was a dreadful sight! I dream of it nights sometimes yet; and he's there in the water, with his wet hair streaming over his eyes, and his eyes sticking out, and his lips blue, fighting the current with one hand, and drifting off, off, inch by inch. all the time. And I wake up with the same longing on me to cry out. 'Let the boy go! Swim! *Swim!*'"

"Well, *did* you cry that?" says Amos.

"Oh no, sir. I went in to him. I pushed a log along and climbed out on it and held out a branch to him, and someway we all got ashore—"

"What did you do with the baby?"

"I was fixing to lay him down in a soft spot when I saw a man was on the bank. He was jumping up and down and yelling: 'I caynt swim a stroke! I caynt swim a stroke!' 'Then you hold the baby,' says I; and I dumped poor Davy into his arms. When we got the boy up the bank he looked plumb dead; but Dave said: 'He ain't dead! He caynt be dead! I won't have him dead!' wild like, and began rubbing him. I ran to the man. If you please, there that unfortunate man was, in the same place, holding Baby as far away from him as he could get, as if he was a dynamite bomb that might go off at any minute. 'Give me your pipe,' says I. 'You will have to fish it out of my pocket yourself,' says he; 'I don't dast loose a hand from this here baby!' And he did look funny! But you may imagine I didn't notice that then. I ran back quick's I could, and we rubbed that boy and worked his arms and, you may say, blowed the breath of life into him. We worked more'n a hour—that poor man holding the baby the enduring time: I reckon *his* arms were stiff's ours! —and I'd have given him up: it seemed awful to be rumpling up a corpse that way. But Dave, he only set his teeth and cried, 'Keep on, I *will* save him!'"

" And you *did* save him ?"

" *He* did," flashed the wife; " he'd be in his grave but for Dave. I'd given him up. And his mother knows it. And she said that if that child was not named Johnny ayfter his paw, she'd name him David ayfter Mist' Brown ; but seeing he was named, she'd do next best, give him David for a middle. And as calling him Johnny David seemed too long, they always call him Johnny D. But won't you rest your hat on the bed and sit down, Mister—"

" Wickliff," finished Amos ; but he added no information regarding his dwelling-place or his walk in life, and, being a Southerner, she did not ask it. By this time she was getting supper ready for the guest. Amos was sure she was a good cook the instant his glance lighted on her snowy and shapely rolls. He perceived that he was to have a much daintier meal than he had ever had before in the "Nation," yet he frowned at the wall. All the innocent, laborious, happy existence of the pair was clear to him as she talked, pleased with so good a listener. The dominant impression which her unconscious confidences made on him was her content.

" I reckon I am a natural-born farmer," she laughed. " I fairly crave to make things grow.

and I love the very smell of the earth and the grass. It's beautiful out here."

"But aren't you ever lonesome ?"

"Why, we've lots of neighbors, and they're all such nice folks. The Robys are awful kind people, and only four miles, and the Atwills are only three, on the other side. And then the Indians drop in, but though I try to be good to them, it's hard to like anybody so dirty. Dave says Red Horse and his band are not fair samples, for they are all young bucks that their fathers won't be responsible for, and they certainly do steal. I don't think they ever stole anything from us, 'cept one hog and three chickens and a jug of whiskey ; but we always feed them well, and it's a little trying, though maybe you'll think I'm inhospitable to say so, to have half a dozen of them drop in and eat up a whole batch of light bread and all the meat you've saved for next day and a plumb jug of molasses at a sitting. That Red Horse is crazy for whiskey, and awful mean when he's drunk : but he's always been civil to us— There's Mist' Brown now !"

Wickliff's first glance at the man in the doorway showed him the same undersized, fair-skinned, handsome young fellow that he remembered ; he wanted to shrug his shoulders and exclaim, "The identical little tough !" but Brown turned his

head, and then Amos was aware that the reck-
lessness and the youth both were gone out of the
face. At that moment it went to the hue of
cigar ashes.

"Here's the gentleman, David; my husband,
Mist' Wickliff," said the wife.

"Papa! papa!" joyously screamed the child,
pattering across the floor. Brown caught the
little thing up and kissed it passionately; and he
held his face for a second against its tiny shoulder
before he spoke (in a good round voice), welcom-
ing his guest. He was too busy with his boy, it
may be, to offer his hand. Neither did Amos
move his arm from his side. He repeated his
errand.

Brown moistened his blue lips; a faint glitter
kindled in his haggard eyes, which went full at
the speaker.

"*That's* what you want, is it?"

"Well, if I want anything more, I'll explain it
on the way," said Amos, unsmilingly.

Brown swallowed something in his throat.
"All right; I guess I can go," said he. "To-
morrow, that is. We can't take pictures by
moonlight; and the road's better by daylight.
Won't you come out with me while I do my
chores? We can—can talk it over." In spite of
his forced laugh there was undisguised entreaty

in his look, and relief when Amos assented. He
went first, saying under his breath, "I suppose
this is how you want."

Amos nodded. They went out, stepping down
the narrow walk between the rows of hollyhocks
to one side and sweet-pease to the other. Amos
turned his head from side to side, against his
will, subdued by the tranquil beauty of the scene.
The air was very still. Only afar, on the river-
bank, the cows were calling to the calves in the
yard. A bell tinkled, thin and sweet, as one cow
waded through the shallow water under the willows. After the dismal neutral tints of the prairie, the rich green of corn-field and grass looked
enchanting, dipped as they were in the glaze of
sunset. The purple-gray of the well-sweep was
painted flatly against a sky of deepest, lustreless
blue—the sapphire without its gleam. But the
river was molten silver, and the tops of the trees
reflected the flaming west, below the gold and
the tumbled white clouds. Turn one way, the
homely landscape held only cool, infinitely soft
blues and greens and grays ; turn the other, and
there burned all the sumptuous dyes of earth and
sky.

"It's a pretty place," said Brown, timidly.

"Very pretty," Amos agreed, without emotion.

"I've worked awfully hard to pay for it. It's all paid for now. You saw my wife."

"Nice lady," said Amos.

"By ——, she is!" The other man swore with a kind of sob. "And she believes in me. We're happy. We're trying to lead a good life."

"I'm inclined to think you're living as decently and lawfully as any citizens of the United States." The tone had not changed.

"Well, what are you going to do?" Brown burst forth, as if he could bear the strain no longer.

"I'm going to do my duty, Harned, and take you to Iowa."

"Will you listen to me first? All you know is, I killed—"

But the officer held up his hand, saying in the same steady voice, "You know whatever you say may be used against you. It's my duty to warn—"

"Oh, I know you, Mr. Wickliff. Come behind the gooseberry bushes where my wife can't see us—"

"It's no use, Harned; if you talked like Bob Ingersoll or an angel, I have to do my duty." Nevertheless he followed, and leaned against the wall of the little shed that did duty for a barn. Harned walked in front of him, too miserably restless to stand still, nervously pulling and breaking wisps of hay between his fingers, talking rapidly, with an earnestness that beaded his forehead and burned in his imploring eyes. " All you know about me " — so he began, quietly enough—"all you know about me is that I was a dissipated, worthless photographer, who could sing a song and had a cursed silly trick of mimicry which made him amusing company ; and so I was trying to keep company with rich fellows. You don't know that when I came to your town I was as innocent a country lad as you ever saw, and had a picture of my dead mother in my Bible, and wrote to my father every week. He was a good man, my father. Lucky he died before he found out about *me*. And you don't know, either, that at first, keeping a little studio on the third story, with a folding - bed in the studio, and doing my cooking on the gas-jet, I was a happy man. But I was. I loved my art. Maybe you don't call a photographer an artist. I do. Because a man works with the sun instead of a brush or a needle, can't he create a picture ? And do you suppose a photographer can't hunt for the soul in a sitter as well as a portrait-painter ? Can't a photographer bring out light and shade in as exquisite gradations as an etcher? Artist ! Any man that can discover beauty, and

can express it in any shape so other men can see
it and love it and be happy on account of it—
he's an artist! And I don't give a damn for a
critic who tries to box up art in his own little
hole!" Harned was excitedly tapping the horny
palm of one hand with the hard, grimy fingers of
the other. Amos thought of the white hands that
he used to take such pains to guard, and then he
looked at the faded check shirt and the patched
overalls. Harned had been a little dandy, too
fond of perfumes and striking styles.

"I was an artist," said Harned. "I loved my
art. I was happy. I had begun to make reputation and money when the devil sent him my
way. He was an amateur photographer; that's
how we got acquainted. When he found I could
sing and mimic voices he was wild over me, flat-
tered me, petted me, taught me all kinds of fool
habits; ruined me, body and soul, with his
friendship. Well, he's dead; and God knows
she wasn't worth a man's life; but he did treat me
mean about her, and when I flew at him he jeered
at me, and he took advantage of my being a little fellow and struck me and cuffed me before
them all; then I went crazy and shot him!" He
stopped, out of breath. Wickliff mused, frowning. The man at his mercy pleaded on, gripping
those slim, roughened hands of his hard togeth-

8

er : "It ain't quite so bad as you thought, is it, Mr. Wickliff? For God's sake put yourself in my place! I went through hell after I shot him. You don't know what it is to live looking over your shoulder! Fear! fear! fear! Day and night, fear! Waking up, maybe, in a cold sweat, hearing some noise, and thinking it meant pursuit and the handcuffs. Why, my heart was jumping out of my mouth if a man clapped me on the shoulder from behind, or hollered across the street to me to stop. Then I met my wife. You need not tell me I had no right to marry. I know it ; I told myself so a hundred times ; but I couldn't leave her alone with her poor old sick father, could I ? And then I found out that— that it would be hard for her, too. And I was all wore out. Man, you don't know what it is to be frightened for two years ? There wasn't a nerve in me that didn't seem to be pulled out as far as it would go. I married her, and we hid ourselves out here in the wilderness. You can say what you please, I have made her happy; and she's made me. If I was to die to-night, she'd thank God for the happy years we've had together ; just as she's thanked Him every night since we were married. The only thing that frets her is me giving up photography. She thinks I could make a name like Wilson or Black. Maybe I could ; but I don't dare ; if I made a reputation I'd be gone. I have to give it up, and do you suppose that ain't a punishment? Do you suppose it's no punishment to sink into obscurity when you know you've got the capacity to do better work than the men that are getting the money and the praise? Do you suppose it doesn't eat into my heart every day that I can't ever give my boy his grandfather's honest name? —that I don't even dare to make his father's name one he would be proud of? Yes, I took his life, but I've given up all my chances in the world for it. My only hope was to change as I grew older and be lost, and the old story would die out—"

" It might ; but you see he had a mother," said Wickliff ; " she offers five thousand—"

" It was only one thousand," interrupted Harned.

" One thousand first year. She's raised a thousand every year. She's a thrifty old party, willing to pay, but not willing to pay any more than necessary. When it got to five thousand I took the case."

Harned looked wistfully about him. " I might raise four thousand—"

" Better stop right there. I refused fifty thousand once to let a man go."

"Excuse me," said Harned, humbly; "I re-member. I'm so distracted I can't think of any-thing but Maggie and the baby. Ain't there anything that will move you? I've paid for that thing. I saved a boy's life once—"

"I know; I've seen the boy."

"Then you know I fought for his life; I fought awful hard. I said to myself, if he lived I'd know it was the sign God had forgiven me. He did live. I've paid, Mr. Wickliff, I've paid in the sight of God. And if it comes to society, it seems to me I'm a good deal more use to it here than I'd be in a State's prison pegging shoes, and my poor wife—"

He choked; but there was no softening of the saturnine gloom of Wickliff's face.

"You ought to tell that all to the lawyer, not to me," said Wickliff. "I'm only a special of-ficer, and my duty is to my employer, not to so-ciety. What's more, I am going to perform it. There isn't anything that can make it right for me to balk on my duty, no matter how sorry I feel for you. No, Mr. Harned, if you live and I live, you go back to Iowa with me."

Harned in utter silence studied the impassive face, and it returned his gaze; then he threw his arm up against the shed, and hid his own face in the crook of his elbow. His shoulders worked

"HARNED HID HIS FACE"

as in a strong shudder, but almost at once they were still, and when he turned his features were blank and steady as the boards behind them.

"I've just one favor to ask," said he; "don't tell my wife. You have got to stay here to-night; it will be more comfortable for you, if I don't say anything till after you've gone to bed. Give me a chance to explain and say good-bye. It will be hard enough for her—"

"Will you give me your parole you won't try to escape?"

"Yes, sir."

"Nor kill yourself?"

Harned started violently, and he laughed. "Do you think I'd kill myself before poor Maggie? I wouldn't be so mean. No, I promise you I won't either run away or kill myself or play any kind of trick on you to-night. Does it go?"

"It goes," responded Amos, holding out his hand; "and I'll give you a good reputation in court, too, for being a good citizen now. That will have weight with the judge. And if you care to know it, I'm mighty sorry for you."

"Thank you, Mr. Wickliff," said Harned; but he had not seemed to see the hand; he was striding ahead.

"That man means to kill himself," thought

Amos : " he's too blamed resigned. He's got it
all planned before. And God help the poor
beggar ! I guess it's the best thing he can do
for himself. Lord, but it's hard sometimes for
a man to do his duty !"

The two men walked along, at first both mute,
but no sooner did they come well in view of the
kitchen door than they began to talk. Amos
hoped there was nothing in the rumors of Indian
troubles.

" There's only one band could make trouble,"
said Harned. " Red Horse is a mean Indian,
educated in the agency schools, and then relapsed.
Say, who's that running up the river - bank ?
Looks like Mrs. Roby's sister. She's got the
baby." His face and voice changed sharply,
he crying out, " There's something wrong with
that woman!" and therewith he set off running
to the house at the top of his speed. Half-way,
Amos, running behind him, could hear a clamor
of women's voices, rising and breaking, and loud
cries. Mrs. Brown came to the doorway, beck-
oning with both hands, screaming for them to
hurry.

When they reached the door they could see the
new - comer. She was huddled in a rocking-
chair, a pitiful, trembling shape, wet to the skin,
her dank cotton skirts dripping, bareheaded, and

her black hair blown about her ghastly face: and on her breast a baby, wet as she, smiling and cooing, but with a great crimson smouch on its tiny shoulder. Near her appeared Johnny D.'s white head. He was pale under his freckles, but he kept assuring her stoutly that uncle wouldn't let the Indians get them.

The woman was so spent with running that her words came in gasps. "Oh, git ready! Fly! They've killed the Robys. They've killed sister and Tom. They killed the children. Oh, my Lord! children! They was clinging to their mother, and crying to the Indians to please not to kill them. Oh, they pretended to be friendly —so's to git in : and we cooked 'em up such a good supper; but they killed every one, little Mary and little Jim—I heard the screeches. I picked up the baby and run. I jumped into the river and swum to the boat—I don't know how I done it—oh, be quick! They'll be coming! Oh, fly!"

Harned turned on Amos. "Flying's no good on land, but maybe the boat—you'll help?"

"Of course," said Amos. "Here, young feller, can you scuttle up to the roof-tree and reconnoitre with this field-glass?—you're considerably lighter on your feet than me. Twist the wheel round here till you can see plain. There's a hole, I see, up to the loft.   Is there one out on the roof ?   Then scuttle!"

Mrs. Brown pushed the coffee back on the stove.   " No use it burning," said she ; and Amos admired her firm tones, though she was deadly pale.   " If we ain't killed we'll need it.   Dave, don't forget the camera.   I'll put up some comforters to wrap the children in and something to eat."   She was doing this with incredible quickness as she spoke, while Harned saw to his gun and the loading of a pistol.

The pistol she took out of his hands, saying, in a low, very gentle voice, " Give that to me, honey."

He gave her a strange glance.

" They sha'n't hurt little Davy or me, Dave," she answered, in the same voice.

Little Davy had gone to the woman and the baby, and was looking about him with frightened eyes ; his lip began to quiver, and he pointed to the baby's shoulder : " Injuns hurt Elly.   Don't let Injuns hurt Davy !"

The wretched father groaned.

" No, baby," said the mother, kissing him.

" Hullo ! up there," called Amos.   " What do you see ?"

The shrill little voice rang back clearly, " They're a-comin', a terrible sight of them."

"How many? Twenty?"

"I guess so. Oh, uncle, the boat's floated off!"

"Didn't you fasten it?" cried Harned.

"God forgive me!" wailed the woman, "I don't know!"

Harned sat down in the nearest chair, and his gun slipped between his knees. "Maggie, give us a drink of coffee," said he, quietly. "We'll have time for that before they come."

"Can't we barricade and fight?" said Amos, glaring about him.

"Then they'll get behind the barn and fire that, and the wind is this way."

"We've *got* to save the women and the kids!" cried Amos. At this moment he was a striking and terrible figure. The veins of his temple swelled with despair and impotent fury; his heavy features were transfigured in the intensity of his effort to think—to see; his arms did not hang at his sides; they were held tensely, with his fist clinched, while his burning eyes roamed over every corner of the room, over every picture. In a flash his whole condition changed, his muscles relaxed, his hands slid into his pockets, he smiled the strangest and grimmest of smiles. "All right," said he. "Ah — Brown. you got any whiskey? Fetch it." The women stared, while Harned passively found a jug and placed it before him.

" Now some empty bottles and tumblers."

" There are some empty bottles in the dark room ; what do you mean to do ?"

" Mean to save you. Brace up ! I'll get them. And you, Mrs. Brown, if you've got any paregoric, give those children a dose that will keep them quiet, and up in the loft with you all. We'll hand up the kids. Listen ! You must keep quiet, and keep the children quiet, and not stir, no matter what infernal racket you may hear down here. You *must!* To save the children. You must wait till you hear one of us, Brown or me, call. See ? I depend on you, and you *must* depend on me !"

Her eyes sought her husband's ; then, " I'm ready, sir," she said, simply. " I'll answer for Johnny D., and the others I'll make quiet."

" That's the stuff," cried Amos, exultantly. " I'll fix the red butchers. Only for God's sake *hustle!*"

He turned his back on the parting to enter the dark room, and when he came back, with his hands full of empty bottles, Harned was alone.

" I told her it was our only chance," said Harned ; " but I'm damned if I know what our only chance is !"

" Never mind that," retorted Amos, briskly. He was entirely calm ; indeed, his face held the kind of grim elation that peril in any shape brings to some natures. " You toss things up and throw open the doors, as if you all had run away in a big fright, while I'll set the table." And, as Harned feverishly obeyed, he carefully filled the bottles from the demijohn. The last bottle he only filled half full, pouring the remains of the liquor into a tumbler.

" All ready ?" he remarked ; " well, here's how," and he passed the tumbler to Harned, who shook his head. " Don't need a brace ? I don't know as you do. Then shake, pardner, and whichever one of us gets out of this all right will look after the women. And — it's all right ?"

"Thank you," choked Harned ; " just give the orders, and I'm there."

" You get into the other room, and you keep there, still ; those are the orders. Don't you come out, whatever you hear ; it's the women's and the children's lives are at stake, do you hear ? And no matter what happens to *me*, you stay *there*, you stay *still!* But the minute I twist the button on that door, let me in, and be ready with your hatchet—that will be handiest. Savez ?"

"Yes ; God bless you, Mr. Wickliff !" cried Harned.

"Pardner it is, now," said Wickliff. They shook hands. Then Harned shut himself in the closet. He did not guess Wickliff's plan, but that did not disturb the hope that was pumping his heart faster. He felt the magnetism of a born leader and an intrepid fighter, and he was Wickliff's to the death. He strained his ears at the door. A chair scraped the boards ; Wickliff was sitting down. Immediately a voice began to sing—Wickliff's voice changed into a tipsy man's maudlin pipe. He was singing a war-song :

"'We'll rally round the flag, boys, we'll rally once
    again,
Shouting the battle-cry of Freedom !' "

The sound did not drown the thud of horses' hoofs outside. They sounded nearer. Then a hail. On roared the song, all on one note. Wickliff couldn't carry a tune to save his soul, and no living man, probably, had ever heard him sing.

"'And we'll drive the savage crew from the land we
    love the best,
Shouting the battle-cry—'

"Hullo ! Who's comin' ? Injuns—mean noble red men ? Come in, gen'lemen all."

The floor shook. They were all crowding in. There was a din of guttural monosyllables and sibilant phrases all fused together, threaten.ng and sinister to the listener; yet he could understand that some of them were of pleasure. That meant the sight of the whiskey.

"P-play fair, gen'lemen," the drunken voice quavered, "thas fine whiskey, fire-water. Got lot. Know where's more. Queer shorter place ever did see. Aller folks skipped. Nobody welcome stranger. Ha, ha !—hic !—stranger found the whiskey, and is shelerbrating for himself. Help yeself, gen'lemen. I know where there's shum—shum more—plenty."

Dimly it came to Harned that here was the man's bid for his life. They wouldn't kill him until he should get the fresh supply of whiskey.

"Where Black Blanket gone ?" grunted Red Horse. Harned knew his voice.

"Damfino," returned the drunken accents, cheerfully. "L-lit out, thas all I know. Whas you mean, hitting each orrer with bottles? Plenty more. I'll go get it. You s-shay where you are."

The blood pounded through Harned's veins at the sound of the shambling step on the floor. His own shoulders involuntarily hunched themselves, quivering as if he felt the tomahawk between them. Would they wait, or would they

shy something at him and kill him the minute
his back was turned ? God! what nerve the
man had ! He was not taking a step the quicker
—ah ! Wickliff's fingers were at the fastening.
He flung the door back. Even then he staggered, keeping to his rôle. But the instant he
was over the threshold the transformation came.
He hurled the door back and threw his weight
against it, quick as a cat. His teeth were set
in a grin of hate, his eyeballs glittered, and he
shook his pistol at the door.

"Come on now, damn you !" he yelled. " We're
ready."

Like an echo to his defiance, there rose an
awful and indescribable uproar from the room
beyond — screams, groans, yells, and simulta-
neously the sound of a rush on the door. But
for a minute the door held.

The clatter of tomahawk blades shook it, but
the wood was thick ; it held.

" Hatchet ready, pard ?" said Wickliff.
" When you feel the door give, slip the bolt to
let 'em tumble in, and then strike for the women
and the kids ; strike hard. I'll empty my pop
into the heap. It won't be such a big one if
the door holds a minute longer."

" What are they doing in there ?" gasped
Harned.

"'IT WON'T BE SUCH A BIG ONE IF THE DOOR HOLDS'"

"They're *dying* in there, that's what," Wickliff replied, between his teeth, "and dying fast. *Now!*"

The words stung Harned's courage into a rush, like whiskey. He shot the bolt, and three Indians tumbled on them, with more—he could not see how many more — behind. Then the hatchet fell. It never faltered after that one glimpse Harned had of the thing at one Indian's belt. He heard the bark of the pistol, twice, three times, the heap reeling; the three foremost were on the floor. He had struck them down too ; but he was borne back. He caught the gleam of the knife lurching at him ; in the same wild glance he saw Wickliff's pistol against a broad red breast, and Red Horse's tomahawk in the air. He struck—struck as Wickliff fired ; struck not at his own assailant, but at Red Horse's arm. It dropped, and Wickliff fired again. He did not see that ; he had whirled to ward the other blow. But the Indian knife made only a random, nerveless stroke, and the Indian pitched forward, doubling up hideously in the narrow space, and thus slipping down—dead.

"That's over !" called Wickliff.

Now Harned perceived that they were standing erect ; they two and only they in the place. Directly in front of them lay Red Horse, the blood streaming from his arm. He was dead; nor was there a single living creature among the Indians. Some had fallen before they could reach the door at which they had flung themselves in the last access of fury; some lay about the floor, and one—the one with the knife—was stiff behind Harned in the dark room.

"Look at that fellow," called Harned. "I didn't hit him; he may be shamming."

"I didn't hit him either," said Wickliff, "but he's dead all the same. So are the others. I'd been too, I guess, but for your good blow on that feller's arm. I saw him, but you can't kill two at once."

"How did you do it?"

"Doped the whiskey. Cyanide of potassium from your photographic drugs; that was the quickest. Even if they had killed you and me, it would work before they could get the women and children. The only risk was their not taking it, and with an Indian that wasn't so much. Now, pardner, you better give a hail, and then we'll hitch up and get them safe in the settlement till we see how things are going."

"And then?" said Harned, growing red.

Amos gnawed at the corners of his mustache in rather a shamefaced way. "Then? Why, then I'll have to leave you, and make the best story I can honestly for the old lady. Oh yes, damn it! I know my duty; I never went back on it before. But I never went back on a pardner either; and after fighting together like we have, I'm not up to any Roman-soldier business; nor I ain't going to give you a pair of handcuffs for saving my life! So run outside and holler to your frau."

Left alone, Wickliff gazed about him in deep meditation, which at last found outlet in a few pensive sentences. "Clean against the rules of war; but rules of war are as much wasted on Injuns as 'please' on a stone-deaf man! And I simply *had* to save the women and children. Still it's a pretty sorry lay-out to pay five thousand dollars for the privilege of seeing. But it's a good deal worse to not do my duty. I shall never forgive myself. But I never should forgive myself for going back on a pardner either. I guess all it comes to is, duty's a cursed blind trail!"

THE HYPNOTIST

THERE were not so many carriages in the little Illinois city with chop-tailed horses, silver chains, and liveried coachmen that the clerks in the big department shop should not know the Courtlandt landau, the Courtlandt victoria, and the Courtlandt brougham (Miss Abbie Courtlandt's private equipage) as well as they knew Madam Courtlandt, Mrs. Etheridge, or Miss Abbie. Two of the shop-girls promptly absorbed themselves in Miss Abbie, one May morning, when she alighted from the brougham. For an instant she stood, as if undecided, looking absently at the window, which happened to be a huge kaleidoscope of dolls.

A tall man and two ragged little girls were staring at the dolls also. Both the girls were miserably thin, and one of them had a bruise on her cheek. The man was much too well clad and prosperous to belong to them. He stroked a drooping black mustache, and said, in the voice of a man accustomed to pet children, whether clean or dirty, "Like these dolls better than yours, sissy?"—at the same time smiling at the girl with the bruised cheek.

A sharp little pipe answered, "I 'ain't got no doll, mister."

"No, she 'ain't," added the other girl; "but *I* got one, only it 'ain't got no right head. Pa stepped on its head. I let her play with it, and we made a head outer a corn-cob. It ain't a very good head."

"I guess not," said the man, putting some silver into her hand; "there, you take that, little sister, and you go in and buy two dolls, one for each of you; and you tell the young lady that waits on you just what you told me. And if there is any money left, you go on over to that bakery and fill up with it."

The children gave him two rapid, bewildered glances, clutched the money, and darted into the store without a word. The man's smiling eyes as they turned away encountered Miss Abbie's, in which was a troubled interest. She had taken a piece of silver from her own purse. He smiled, as perceiving a kindly impulse that matched his own; and she, to her own later surprise, smiled too. The smile changed in a flash

to a startled look ; all the color drifted out of
her face, and she took a step forward so hastily that she stumbled on her skirt. Recovering
herself, she dropped her purse ; and a man who
had just approached went down on one knee to
pick it up. But the tall man was too quick for
him ; a long arm swooped in between the other's
outstretched hand and the gleaming bit of liz-
ard-skin on the bricks. The new-comer barely
avoided a collision. He did not take the escape
with good-humor, scowling blackly as he made a
scramble, while still on his knee, at something
behind the tall man's back. This must have
been a handkerchief, since he immediately presented a white flutter to Miss Courtlandt, bowing and murmuring, " You dropped this too, I
guess, madam."

" Yes, thank you," stammered Miss Courtlandt ; " thank you very much, Mr. Slater."
She entered the store by his side, but at the
door she turned her head for a parting nod of
acknowledgment to the other. He remained a
second longer, staring at the dolls, and gnaw-
ing the ends of his mustache, not irritated, but
sharply thoughtful.

Thus she saw him, glancing out again, once
more, when inside the store. And through all
the anguish of the moment—for she was in a

dire strait—she felt a faint pang that she should have been rude to this kind stranger. In a feeble way she wondered, as they say condemned criminals wonder at street sights on the way to the gallows, what he was thinking of. But had he spoken his thought aloud she had not been the wiser, since he was simply saying softly to himself, " Well, wouldn't it kill you dead !"

Miss Abbie stopped at the glove-counter to buy a pair of gloves. As she walked away she heard distinctly one shop-girl's sigh and exclamation to the other, " My, I wish I was her !"

A kind of quiver stirred Miss Abbie's faded cold face. Her dark gray eyes recoiled sidewise; then she stiffened from head to heel and passed out of the store.

To a casual observer she looked annoyed ; in reality she was both miserable and humiliated. And once back in the shelter of the brougham her inward torment showed plainly in her face.

Abigail Courtlandt was the second daughter of the house; never so admired as Mabel, the oldest, who died, or Margaret, the youngest, who married Judge Etheridge, and was now a widow, living with her widowed mother.

Abigail had neither the soft Hayward loveliness of Mabel and her mother, nor the haughty beauty of Margaret, who was all a Courtlandt, yet she was not uncomely. If her chin was too long, her forehead too high, her ears a trifle too large, to offset these defects she had a skin of exquisite texture, pale and clear, white teeth, and beautiful black brows.

She was thin, too thin ; but her dressmaker was an artist, and Abbie would have been graceful were she not so nervous, moving so abruptly, and forever fiddling at something with her fingers. When she sat next any one talking, it did not help that person's complacency to have her always sink slightly on the elbow further from her companion, as if averting her presence. An embarrassed little laugh used to escape her at the wrong moment. Withal, she was cold and stiff, although some keen people fancied that her coldness and stiffness were no more than a mask to shield a morbid shyness. These same people said that if she would only forget herself and become interested in other people she would be a lovable woman, for she had the kindest heart in the world. Unfortunately all her thoughts concentred on herself. Like many shy people, Abbie was vain. Diffidence as often comes from vanity, which is timid, as from self - distrust. Abbie longed passionately not only to be loved, but to be admired. She was loved, assuredly, but she was not especially admired. Margaret

Etheridge, with her courage, her sparkle, and her beauty, was always the more popular of the sisters. Margaret was imperious, but she was generous too, and never oppressed her following; only the rebels were treated to those stinging speeches of hers. Those who loved Margaret admired her with enthusiasm. No one admired poor Abbie with enthusiasm. She was her father's favorite child, but he died when she was in short dresses; and, while she was dear to all the family, she did not especially gratify the family pride.

Her hungry vanity sought refuge in its own creations. She busied herself in endless fictions of reverie, wherein an imaginary husband and an imaginary home of splendor appeased all her longings for triumph. While she walked and talked and drove and sewed, like other people, only a little more silent, she was really in a land of dreams.

Did her mother complain because she had forgotten to send the Book Club magazines or books to the next lawful reader, she solaced herself by visions of a book club in the future which she and "he" would organize, and a reception of distinguished elegance which "they" would give, to which the disagreeable person who made a fuss over nothing (meaning the reader to whom reading was due) should not be invited—thereby reducing her to humility and tears. But even the visionary tears of her offender affected Abbie's soft nature, and all was always forgiven.

Did Margaret have a swarm of young fellows disputing over her card at a ball, while Abbie must sit out the dances, cheered by no livelier company than that of old friends of the family, who kept up a water-logged pretence of conversation that sank on the approach of the first new-comer or a glimpse of their own daughters on the floor, Abbie through it all was dreaming of the balls "they" would give, and beholding herself beaming and gracious amid a worshipping throng.

These mental exercises, this double life that she lived, kept her inexperienced. At thirty she knew less of the world than a girl in her first season; and at thirty she met Ashton Clarke. Western society is elastic, or Clarke never would have been on the edges even; he never did get any further, and his morals were more dubious than his position; but he was Abbie's first impassioned suitor, and his flattering love covered every crack in his manners or his habits. Men had asked her to marry them before, but never had a man made love to her. For two weeks she was a happy woman. Then came discovery, and the storm broke. The Courtlandts were in a rage—except gentle Madam Courtlandt, who was broken-hearted and ashamed, which was worse for Abbie. Jack, the older brother, was summoned from Chicago. Ralph, the younger, tore home on his own account from Yale. It was really a testimony to the family's affection for Abbie that she created such a commotion, but it did not impress her in that way. In the end she yielded, but she yielded with a sense of cruel injustice done her.

Time proved Clarke worse than her people's accusations; but time did not efface what the boys had said, much less what the girls had said. They forgot, of course; it is so much easier to forget the ugly words that we say than those that are said to us. But she remembered that Jack felt that Abbie never did have any sense, and that Ralph raged because she did not even know a cad from a gentleman, and that Margaret, pacing the floor, too angry to sit still, would not have minded so much had Abbie made a fool of herself for a *man;* but she didn't wait long enough to discover what he was; she positively accepted the first thing with a mustache on it that offered !

Time healed her heart, but not her crushed and lacerated vanity. And it is a question whether we do not suffer more keenly, if less deeply, from wounds to the self-esteem than to the heart. Generally we mistake the former for the latter, and declare ourselves to have a sensitive heart, when what we do have is only a thin-skinned vanity!

But there was no mistake about Abbie's misery, however a moralist might speculate concerning the cause. She suffered intensely. And she had no confidant. She had not even her old fairyland of fancy, for love and lovers were become hateful to her. At first she went to church—until an unlucky difference with the rector's wife at a church fair. Later it was as much her unsatisfied vanity and unsatisfied heart as any spiritual confusion that led her into all manner of excursions into the shadowy border-land of the occult. She was a secret attendant on table-tippings and séances; a reader of every kind of mystical lore that she could buy; an habitual consulter of spiritual mediums and clairvoyants and seventh sons and daughters and the whole tribe of charlatans. But the family had not noticed. They were not afraid of the occult ones; they were glad to have Abbie happy and more contented; and they concerned themselves no further, as is the manner of families, being occupied with their own concerns.

And so unguarded Abbie went to her evil fate. One morning, with her maid Lucy, she went to see "the celebrated clairvoyant and seer, Professor Rudolph Slater, the greatest revealer of the future in this or any other century."

Lucy looked askance at the shabby one-story saloons on the street, and the dying lindens before the house. Her disapproval deepened as they went up the wooden steps. The house was one of a tiny brick block, with wooden cornices, and unshaded wooden steps in need not only of painting but scrubbing.

The door opened into an entry which was dark, but not dark enough to conceal the rents in the oil-cloth on the floor or the blotches on the imitation oak paper of the walls.

Lucy sniffed; she was a faithful and affectionate attendant, and she used considerable freedom with her mistress. "I don't know about there being spirits here, but there's been lots of onions!" remarked Lucy. Nor did her unfavorable opinion end with the approach to the sorcerer's presence. She maintained her wooden expression even sitting in the great man's room and hearing his speech.

Abbie did not see the hole in the green rep covering of the arm-chair, nor the large round oil-stain on the faded roses of the carpet, nor the dust on the Parian ornaments of the table; she was too absorbed in the man himself.

If his surroundings were sordid, he was splendid in a black velvet jacket and embroidered shirt-front sparkling with diamonds. He was a short man, rather thick-set, and although his hair was gray, his face was young and florid. The gray hair was very thick, growing low on his forehead and curling. Abbie thought it beautiful. She thought his eyes beautiful also, and spoke to Lucy of their wonderful blue color and soul-piercing gaze.

"I thought they were just awful impudent," said Lucy. "I never did see a man stare so, Miss Abbie; I wanted to slap him!"

"But his hair *was* beautiful," Abbie persisted; "and he said it used to be straight as a poker, but the spirits curled it."

"Why, Miss Abbie," cried Lucy, "I could see the little straight ends sticking out of the curls, that come when you do your hair up on irons. I've frizzed my hair too many times not to know *them*."

"But, Lucy," said Abbie, in a low, shocked voice, "didn't you feel *something* when he put on those handcuffs and sat before the cabinet in the dark, and his control spoke, and we saw the hands? What do you think of that?"

"I think it was him all the time," said Lucy, doggedly.

"But, Lucy, *why?*"

"Finger-nails were dirty just the same," said Lucy. Nor was there any shaking her. But Abbie, under ordinary circumstances the most fastidious of women, had not noted the finger-nails; one witching sentence had captured her.

The moment he took her hand he had started violently. "Excuse me, madam," said he, "but are you not a medium *yourself?*"

"No—at least, I never was supposed to be," fluttered Abbie, blushing.

"Then, madam, you don't perhaps realize that you yourself possess marvellous psychic power. I never saw any one who had so much, when it had not been developed."

To-day Abbie ground her teeth and wrung her hands in an impotent agony of rage, remembering her pleasure. He would not take any money; no, he said, there had been too much happiness for him in meeting such a favorite of the spiritual influences as she.

"But you will come again," he pleaded; "only don't ask me to take money for such a great privilege. *You* caynt see the invisible guardians that hover around you!"

His refusal of her gold piece completed his

victory over Abbie's imagination. She was sure
he could not be a cheat, since he would not be
paid. She did come again; she came many
times, always with Lucy, who grew more and
more suspicious, but could not make up her
mind to expose Abbie's folly to her people.
"Think of all the things she gives me!" argued
Lucy. "Miss Abbie's always been a kind of
stray sheep in the family; they are all kind of
hard on her. I can't bear to be the one to get
her into trouble."

So Lucy's conscience squirmed in silence until
the fortune-teller persuaded Abbie to allow him
to throw her into a trance. The wretched woman in the carriage cowered back farther into the
shade, living over that ghastly hour when Lucy
at her elbow was as far away from her helpless
soul as if at the poles. How his blue eyes
glowed! How the flame in them contracted to
a glittering spark, like the star-tip of the silver
wand, waving and curving and interlacing its
dazzling flashes before her until her eyeballs
ached! How of a sudden the star rested, blink-
ing at her between his eyes, and she looked; she
must look at it, though her will, her very self,
seemed to be sucked out of her into the gleaming whirlpool of that star!

She made a feeble rally under a woful im-

10

pression of fright and misery impending, but in
vain ; and, with the carelessness of a creature
who is chloroformed, she let her soul drift
away.

When she opened her eyes, Lucy was rubbing
her hands, while the clairvoyant watched the two
women motionless and smiling.

The fear still on her prompted her first words,
" Let me go home now !"

" Not now," begged the conjurer ; "you must
go into a trance again.   I want you to see something that will be very interesting to you.   Please,
Miss Courtlandt."   He spoke in the gentlest of
tones, but there was a repressed assurance about
his manner that was infuriating to Lucy.

" Miss Abbie's going home," she cried, an-
grily ; "we ain't going to have any more of this
nonsense.   Come, Miss Abbie."   She touched
her on her arm, but trembling Abbie fixed her
eyes on the conjurer, and he, in that gentle
tone, answered :

" Certainly, if she wishes ; but she *wants* to
stay.   You want to stay, Miss Courtlandt, don't
you ?"

"Yes, I want to stay," said Abbie ; and her
heart was cold within her, for the words seemed
to say themselves, even while she struggled frantically against the utterance of them.

"'SHE MUST LOOK AT IT'"

"Do you mean it, Miss Abbie?" the girl repeated, sorely puzzled.

"Certainly, just once more," said Miss Abbie. And she sat down again in her chair.

What she saw she never remembered. Lucy said it was all nonsense she talked, and, anyhow, she whispered so low that nobody could catch more than a word, except that she seemed to be promising something over and over again. In a little while the conjurer whispered to her, and with a few passes of his hand consciousness returned. She rose, white and shaken, but quite herself again. He bade the two good-bye, and bowed them out with much suavity of manner. Abbie returned not a single word. As they drove home, the maid spoke, "Miss Abbie, Miss Abbie—you won't go there again, will you?"

"Never," cried Abbie—"never!"

But the next morning, after a sleepless night, there returned the same horrible, dragging longing to see him; and with the longing came the same fear that had suffocated her will the day before—a fear like the fear of dreams, formless, reasonless, more dreadful than death.

Impelled by this frightful force that did not seem to have anything to do with her, herself, she left the house and boarded a street-car. She felt as if a demon were riding her soul, spur-

ring it wherever he willed. She went to a little
park outside the city, frequented by Germans
and almost deserted of a week-day. And on
her way she remembered that this was what she
had promised him to do.

He was waiting to assist her from the car. As
he helped her alight, she noticed his hands and
his nails. They were neat enough; yet she
suddenly recalled Lucy's words; and suddenly
she saw the man, in his tasteless, expensive
clothes, with his swagger and the odor of whiskey about him, as any other gentlewoman would
have seen him. Her fright had swept all his
seer's glamour away; he was no longer the mystical ruler of the spirit-world; he was a squalid
adventurer—and her master !

He made her realize that in five minutes.
"You caynt help yourself, Miss Courtlandt,"
he said, and she believed him.

Whether it were the influence of a strong will
on a hysterical temperament and a morbidly im-
pressible fancy, or whether it were a black power
from the unseen, beyond his knowledge but not
beyond his abuse, matters little so far as poor
Abbie Courtlandt was concerned; on either sup-
position, she was powerless.

She left him, hating him as only slavery and
fear can hate; but she left him pledged to bring

him five hundred dollars in the morning and to marry him in the afternoon ; and now, having kept her word about the money, she was driving home, clinching in her cold fingers the slip of paper containing the address of a justice of the peace in the suburbs, where she must meet him and be bound to this unclean vulture, who would bear her away from home and kindred and all fair repute and peace.

A passion of revolt shook her. She *must* meet him ? Why must she ? Why not tear his address to bits ? Why not drive fast, fast home, and tell her mother that she was going to Chicago about some gowns that night ? Why not stay there at Jack's, and let this fiend, who harried her, wait in vain ? She twisted the paper and ground her teeth ; yet she knew that she shouldn't tear it, just as we all know we shall not do the frantic things that we imagine, even while we are finishing up the minutest details the better to feign ourselves in earnest. Poor, weak Abbie knew that she never would dare to confess her plight to her people. No, she could never endure another family council of war.

"There is only one way," she muttered. Instead of tearing the paper she read it :

" *Be at Squire L. B. Leitner's, 398 S. Miller Street, at 3 p.m. sharp.*"

And now she did tear the odious message, flinging the pieces furiously out of the carriage window.

The same tall, dark, square-shouldered man that she had seen in front of the shop-window was passing, and immediately bent and picked up some of the shreds. For an instant the current of her terror turned, but only for an instant. What could a stranger do with an address?" She sank into the corner, and her miserable thoughts harked back to the trap that held her.

Like one in a nightmare, she sat, watching the familiar sights of the town drift by, to the accompaniment of her horses' hoofs and jingling chains. "This is the last drive I shall ever take," she thought.

She felt the slackening of speed, and saw (still in her nightmare) the broad stone steps and the stately, old-fashioned mansion, where the daintiest of care and the trimmest of lawns had turned the old ways of architecture from decrepitude into pride.

Lunch was on the table, and her mother nodded her pretty smile as she passed. Abbie had a box of flowers in her hand, purchased earlier in the morning; these she brought into the dining-room. There were violets for her mother and American Beauties for Margaret. "They looked so sweet I had to buy them," she half apologized. Going through the hall, she heard her mother say, "How nice and thoughtful Abbie has grown lately!" And Margaret answered, "Abbie is a good deal more of a woman than I ever expected her to be."

All her life she had grieved because—so she morbidly put it to herself—her people despised her; now that it was too late, was their approval come to her only to be flung away with the rest? She returned to the dining-room and went through the farce of eating. She forced herself to swallow; she talked with an unnatural ease and fluency. Several times her sister laughed at her words. Her mother smiled on her fondly. Margaret said, "Abbie, why can't you go to Chicago with me to-night and have a little lark? You have clothes to fit, too; Lucy can pack you up, and we can take the night train."

"I *would*," chimed in Mrs. Courtlandt. "You look so ill, Abbie. I think you must be bilious; a change will be nice for you. And I'll ask Mrs. Curtis over for a few days while you are gone, and we will have a little tea-party of our own and a little lark for ourselves."

Never before had Margaret wished Abbie to accompany her on "a little lark." Abbie assented like a person in a dream; only she must go down to the bank after luncheon, she said.

Up-stairs in her own chamber she gazed about the pretty furnishings with blank eyes. There was the writing-desk that her mother gave her Christmas, there glistened the new dressing-table that Margaret helped her about finishing, and there was the new paper with the sprawly flowers that she thought so ugly in the pattern, and took under protest, and liked so much on the walls. How often she had been unjust to her people, and yet it had turned out that they were right! Her thoughts rambled on through a thousand memories, stumbling now into pitfalls of remorse over long-forgotten petulance and ingratitude and hardenings of her heart against kindness, again recovering and thread-ing some narrow way of possible release, only to sink as the wall closed again hopelessly about her.

For the first time she arraigned her own vanity as the cause of her long unhappiness. Well, it was no use now. All she could do for them would be to drift forever out of their lives. She opened the drawer, and took a vial from a secret corner. "It is only a little faintness and numb-ness, and then it is all over," she thought, as she slipped the vial into the chatelaine bag at her waist. In a sudden gust of courage she took it out again; but that instinctive trusting to hope to the last, which urges the most desperate of us on delay, held her hand. She put back the vial, and, without a final glance, went down the stairs. It was in her heart to have one more look at her mother, but at the drawing-room door she heard voices, and happening to glance up at the clock, she saw how near the time the hour was; so she hurried through the hall into the street.

During the journey she hardly felt a distinct thought. But at intervals she would touch the outline of the vial at her waist.

The justice's office was in the second story of a new brick building that twinkled all over with white mortar. Below, men laughed, and glasses and billiard-balls clicked behind bright new green blinds. A steep, dark wooden stairway, apparently trodden by many men who chewed tobacco and regarded the world as their cuspidor, led between the walls up to a narrow hall, at the farther end of which a door showed on its glass panels the name L. B. Leitner, J.P.

Abbie rapped feebly on the glass, to see the door instantly opened by Slater himself. He had donned a glossy new frock-coat and a white tie. His face was flushed.

"I didn't intend you should have to enter

here alone," he exclaimed, drawing her into the
room with both hands; "I was jest going outside to wait for you. Allow me to introduce
Squire Leitner. Squire, let me make you ac·
quainted with Miss Courtlandt, the lady who will
do me the honor."

He laughed a little nervous laugh. He was
plainly affecting the manner of the fortunate
bridegroom, and not quite at ease in his rôle.
Neither of the two other men in the room returned any answering smile.

The justice, a bald, gray-bearded, kindly, and
worried-looking man, bowed and said, "Glad to
meet you, ma'am," in a tone as melancholy as
his wrinkled brow.

"Squire is afraid you are not here with your
own free-will and consent, Abbie," said Slater,
airily; "but I guess you can relieve his mind."

At the sound of her Christian name (which
he had never pronounced before) Abbie turned
white with a sort of sick disgust and shame.
But she raised her eyes and met the intense gaze
of the tall, dark man that she had seen before.
He stood, his elbow on the high desk and his
square, clean-shaven chin in his hand. He was
neatly dressed, with a rose in his button-hole,
and an immaculate pink-and-white silk shirt;
but he hardly seemed (to Abbie) like a man of

her own class. Nevertheless, she did not resent his keen look ; on the contrary, she experienced a sudden thrill of hope—something of the same feeling she had known years and years ago, when she ran away from her nurse, and a big policeman found her, both her little slippers lost in the mud of an alley, she wailing and paddling along in her stocking feet, and carried her home in his arms.

"Yes, Miss Courtlandt"—she winced at the voice of the justice —"it is my duty under the—hem—unusual circumstances of this case, to ask you if you are entering into this— hem — solemn contract of matrimony, which is a state honorable in the sight of God and man, by the authority vested in me by the State of Illinois—hem—to ask you if you are entering it of your own free-will and consent—are you, miss ?"

Abbie's sad gray eyes met the magistrate's look of perplexed inquiry ; her lips trembled.

"Are you, Abbie ?" said the clairvoyant, in a gentle tone.

"Yes," answered Abbie ; "of my own free-will and consent."

"I guess, professor, I must see the lady alone," said the justice, dryly.

"You caynt believe it is a case of true love

laffs at the aristocrats, can you, squire ?" sneered
Slater ; " but jest as she pleases. Are you willing to see him, Abbie ?"

" Whether Miss Courtlandt is willing or not,"
interrupted the tall man, in a mellow, leisurely
voice, " I guess *I* will have to trouble you for a
small ' sceance' in the other room, Marker."

"And who are you, sir ?" said Slater, civilly,
but with a truculent look in his blue eyes.

" This is Mr. Amos Wickliff, of Iowa, special
officer," the justice said, waving one hand at the
man and the other at Abbie.

Wickliff bowed in Abbie's direction, and sa-
luted the fortune-teller with a long look in his
eyes, saying :

" Wasn't Bill Marker that I killed out in Ari-
zona your cousin ?"

"My name ain't Marker, and I never had a
cousin killed by you or anybody," snapped back
the fortune-teller, in a bigger and rounder voice
than he had used before.

Wickliff merely narrowed his bright black eyes,
opened a door, and motioned within, saying,
" Better."

The fortune - teller scowled, but he walked
through the door, and Wickliff, following, closed
it behind him.

Abbie looked dumbly at the justice. He sighed, rubbed his hands together, and placed a chair against the wall.

"There's a speaking-tube hole where we used to have a tube, but I took it out, 'cause it was too near the type-writer," said he. "It's just above the chair; if you put your ear to that hole I guess it would be the best thing. You can place every confidence in Mr. Wickliff; the chief of police here knows him well; he's a perfect gentleman, and you don't need to be afraid of hearing any rough language. No, ma'am."

Abbie's head swam ; she was glad to sit down. Almost mechanically she laid her ear to the hole.

The first words audible came from Wickliff. "Certainly I will arrest you. And I'll take you to Toronto to-night, and you can settle with the Canadian authorities about things. Rosenbaum offers a big reward ; and Rosenbaum, I judge, is a good fellow, who will act liberally."

"I tell you I'm not Marker," cried Slater, fiercely, "and it wouldn't matter a damn if I was ! Canada ! You caynt run a man in for Canada !"

Wickliff chuckled. "Can't I ?" said he ; "that's where you miss it, Marker. Now I haven't any time to fool away ; you can take your choice : go off peacefully—I've a hack at the door — and we'll catch the 5:45 train for Toronto, and there you shall have all the law and justice you want; or you can just make one step towards that door, or one sound, and I'll slug you over the head, and load you into the carriage neatly done up in chloroform, and when you wake up you'll be on the train with a decent gentleman who doesn't know anything about international law, but does know *me*, and wouldn't turn his head if you hollered bloody murder. See ?"

" That won't go down. You caynt kidnap me that way! I'll appeal to the squire. No, no! I *won't!* Before God, I won't—I was jest fooling !"

The voice of terror soothed Abbie's raw nerves like oil on a burn. " He's scared now, the coward !" she rejoiced, savagely.

"There's where we differ, then," retorted Wickliff ; " *I* wasn't."

" That's all right. Only one thing : will you jest let me marry my sweetheart before I go, and I'll go with you like a holy lamb ; I will, by—"

" No swearing, Marker. That lady don't want to marry you, and she ain't going to—"

"*Ask* her," pleaded Slater, desperately. " I'll leave it with her. If she don't say she loves me and wants to marry me, I'll go all right."

Abbie's pulses stood still.

" Been trying the hypnotic dodge again, have

"'HE'S SCARED NOW, THE COWARD'"

you ?" said Wickliff, contemptuously. "Well, it won't work this time. I've got too big a curl on you."

There was a pause the length of a heart-beat, and then the hated tones, shrill with fear: "I *wasn't* going to the window! I wasn't going to speak—"

"See here," the officer's iron-cold accents interrupted, "let us understand each other. Rosenbaum hates you, and good reason, too; *he'd* much rather have you dead than alive; and you ought to know that *I* wouldn't mind killing you any more than I mind killing a rat. Give me a good excuse—pull that pop you have in your inside pocket just a little bit—and you're a stiff one, sure! See?"

Again the pause, then a sullen voice: "Yes, damn you! I see. Say, won't you let me say good-bye to my girl?"

Abbie clinched her finger-nails into her hands during the pause that followed. Wickliff's reply was a surprise; he said, musingly, "Got any money out of her, I wonder?"

"I swear to God not a red cent!" cried the conjurer, vehemently.

"Oh, you *are* a scoundrel, and no mistake," laughed Wickliff. "That settles it; you *have!* Well, I'll call her—Oh, Miss Courtlandt!"—he

elevated his soft tones to a roaring bellow—
"please excuse my calling you, and step out
here! Or we'll go in there."

"If it's anything private, you'll excuse me,"
interposed a mild voice at her elbow; and when
she turned her head, behold a view of the skirts
of the minister of justice as he slammed a door
behind him!

A second later, Wickliff entered, propelling
Slater by the shoulder.

"Ah! Squire stepped out a moment, has he?"
said the officer, blandly. "Well, that makes it
awkward, but I may as well tell you, madam,
with deep regret, that this man here is a professional swindler, who is most likely a bigamist
as well, and he has done enough mischief for a
dozen, in his life. I'm taking him to Canada
now for a particularly bad case of hypnotic influence and swindling, etc. Has he got any
money out of you?" As he spoke he fixed his
eyes on her. "Don't be afraid if he has hyp-
notized you; he won't try those games before
me. Kindly turn your back on the lady, Johnny." (As he spoke he wheeled the fortune-teller
round with no gentle hand.) "He has? How
much?"

It was strange that she should no longer feel
afraid of the man; but his face, as he cowered

under the heavy grasp of the officer, braced her courage. "He has five hundred dollars I gave him this morning," she cried; "but he may keep it if he will only let me go. I don't want to marry him!"

"Of course you don't, a lady like you! He's done the same game with nice ladies before. Keep your head square, Johnny, or I'll give your neck a twist! And as to the money, you'll march out with me to the other room, and you'll fish it out, and the lady will kindly allow you fifty dollars of it for your tobacco while you're in jail in Canada. That's enough, Miss Courtlandt—more would be wasted—and if he doesn't be quick and civil, I'll act as his valet."

The fortune-teller wheeled half round in an excess of passion, his fingers crooked on their way to his hip pocket; then his eye ran to the officer, who had simply doubled his fist and was looking at the other man's neck. Instinctively Slater ducked his head; his hand dropped.

"No, no, please," Miss Courtlandt pleaded; "*let* him keep it, if he will only go away."

"Beg pardon, miss," returned the inflexible Wickliff, "you're only encouraging him in bad ways. Step, Johnny."

"If you'll let me have that five hundred,"

11

cried Slater, " I'll promise to go with you, though you know I have the legal right to stay."

" You'll go with me as far as you have to, and no farther, promise or no promise," said Wickliff, equably. " You're a liar from Wayback! And I'm letting you keep that revolver a little while so you may give me a chance to kill you. Step, now !"

Slater ground his teeth, but he walked out of the room.

" At least, give him a hundred dollars !" begged Miss Courtlandt as the door closed. In a moment it opened again, and the two re-entered. Slater's wrists were in handcuffs ; nevertheless, he had reassumed a trifle of his old jaunty bearing, and he bowed politely to Abbie, proffering her a roll of bills. " There are four hundred there, Miss Courtlandt," said he. " I am much obliged to you for your generosity, and I assure you I will never bother you again." He made a motion that she knew, with his shackled hands. " You are quite free from me," said he ; " and, after all, you will consider that it was only the money you lost from me. I always treated you with respect, and to-day was the only day I ever made bold to speak of you or to you by your given name. Good-bye, Miss Courtlandt ; you're a real lady, and I'll tell you now it was all a fake

" 'I'LL ACT AS HIS VALET' "

about the spirits. I guess there are real spirits
and real mediums, but they didn't any of 'em
ever fool with *me*. Good-afternoon, ma'am."

Abigail took the notes mechanically; he had
turned and was at the door before she spoke.
" God forgive you !" said she. " Good-bye."

"That was a decent speech, Marker," said
Wickliff, "and you'll see I'll treat you decent
on the way. Good-morning, Miss Courtlandt.
I needn't say, I guess, that no one will know
anything of this little matter from the squire or
me, not even the squire's wife. *I* 'ain't got one.
I wish you good-morning, ma'am. No, ma'am "
—as she made a hurried motion of the money
towards him—" I shall get a large reward ; don't
think of it, ma'am. But if you felt like doing
the civil thing to the squire, a box of cigars is
what any gentleman is proud to receive from a
lady, and I should recommend leaving the brand
to the best cigar-store you know. Good-morning, ma'am."

Barely were the footsteps out of the hall when
the worthy justice, very red and dusty, bounced
out of the closet. " Excuse me," gasped he,
"but I couldn't stand it a minute longer ! Sit
down, Miss Courtlandt ; and don't, please, think
of fainting, miss, for I'm nearly smothered myself !" He bustled to the water-cooler, and prof-

fered water, dripping over a tin cup on to Abbie's
hands and gown; and he explained, with that air
of intimate friendliness which is a part of the
American's mental furniture, "I thought it better to let Wickliff *persuade him* by himself.   He
is a remarkable man, Amos Wickliff; I don't suppose there's a special officer west of the Missis-
sippi is his equal for arresting bad cases.   And
do you know, ma'am, he never was after this
Marker.   Just come here on a friendly visit to
the chief of police.   All he knew of Marker was
from the newspapers; he had been reading the
letter of the man Marker swindled in Canada,
and his offer of a reward for him.   Marker's
picture was in it, and a description of his hair
and all his looks, and Wickliff just picked him
out from that.   I call that pretty smart, picking up a man from his picture in a newspaper.
Why, I "—he assumed a modest expression, but
glowed with pride—"*I* have had my picture in
the paper, and my wife didn't know it.   Yes,
ma'am, Wickliff is at the head of the profession,
and no mistake!   Didn't have a sign of a warrant.   Just jumped on the job; telegraphed for
a warrant to meet him at Toronto."

"But will he take him safely to Canada?"
stammered Miss Abigail.

"Not a doubt of it," said the justice.   And it

may be mentioned here that his prediction came true. Wickliff sent a telegram the next day to the chief of police, announcing his safe arrival.

Miss Courtlandt went to Chicago by the evening train. She is a happier woman, and her family often say, "How nice Abbie is growing!" She has never seen the justice since; but when his daughter was married the whole connection marvelled and admired over a trunk of silver that came to the bride—"From one to whom her father was kind."

The only comment that the justice made was to his wife: "Yes, my dear, you're right; it *is* a woman, a lady; but if you knew all about it, how I never saw her but the once, and all, you wouldn't mind Bessie's taking it. She was a nice lady, and I'm glad to have obliged her. But it really ought to go to another man."

THE NEXT ROOM

THE NEXT ROOM

IT was as much the mystery as the horror that made the case of Margaret Clark (commonly known as Old Twentypercent) of such burning interest to the six daily journals of the town. I have been told that the feet of tireless young reporters wore a separate path up the bluff to the site of old Margaret's abode ; but this I question, because there were already two paths made for them by the feet of old Margaret's customers—the winding path up the grassy slope, and the steps hewn out of the sheer yellow bluffside, sliced down to make a backing for the street. These are the facts that, whichever the path taken, they were able to glean: Miss Margaret lived on the bluff in the western part of town. The street below crosses at right angles the street running to the river, which is of the kind the French term an "impasse." It is a street of varied fortunes, beginning humbly in a wide and tree-

less plain, where jimson, dock, and mustard weed
have their will with the grass, passing a number
of houses, each in its own tiny yard, creeping up
the hill and the social scale at the same time, until
it is bordered by velvety boulevards and terraces
and lawns that glow in the evening light, and
pretty houses often painted ; then dropping again
to a lonely gully, with the flaming kilns of the
brick-yard on one side, and the huge dark bulk
of the brewery on the other, reaching at last the
bustle and roar of the busiest street in town.
The great arc-light swung a dazzling white porcupine above the brewery vats every night (when
the moon did not shine), and hung level with
the crest of the opposite bluff.   By day or night
one could see the trim old-fashioned garden and
the close-cropped lawn and the tall bur-oaks that
shaded the two-story brown cottage in which for
fifteen years Margaret Clark had lived.   Here
she was living at the time of these events, with
no protector except her bull-dog, the Colonel
(who, to be sure, understood his business, and I
cannot deny him a personal pronoun), and no
companion except Esquire Clark, her cat.   She
did not keep fowls—judging it right and necessary to slay them on occasion, but never having
the heart to kill anything for which she had
cared and which she had taught to know her.

Therefore she bought her eggs and her "frying chickens" of George Washington, a worthy colored man who lived below the hill, and who kept Margaret's garden in order. Although he had worked for her (satisfactory service given for satisfactory wage) during all these fifteen years, he knew as little about her, he declared, as the first week he came. Nor did the wizened little Irishwoman who climbed the clay stairway three times a week to wash and scrub know any more. But she stoutly maintained "the old lady was a rale lady, and the saints would be good to her." One reporter, more curious, discovered that Margaret several times had helped this woman over a rough pass.

The only other person (outside of her customers) who kept so much as a speaking acquaintance with Margaret was the sheriff, Amos Wickliff. And what he knew of her he was able to keep even from the press. As for the customers, her malicious nickname explains her business. Margaret was an irregular money-lender. She loaned money for short periods on personal security or otherwise. It should speak well for her shrewdness that she rarely made a bad debt. Yet she was not unpopular; on the contrary, she had the name of giving the poor a long day, and, for one of her trade, was esteemed lenient.

Shortly after her accident, also (she had the ill-hap to fall down her cellar-way, injuring her spine), she had remitted a number of debts to her poorest debtors.

The accident occurred of a Wednesday morning; Wednesday afternoon her nephew called on her, having, he said, but just discovered her whereabouts. The reporters discovered that this nephew, Archibald Cary Allerton by name, was not an invited and far from a welcome guest, although he gave out that his mother and he were his aunt's sole living kindred. She would not speak to him when he visited her, turning her head to the wall, moaning and muttering, so that it was but kindness to leave her. The nurse (Mrs. Raker, the jailer's wife, had come up from the jail) said that he seemed distressed. He called again during the evening, after Wickliff, who spent most of the evening with her alone, was gone, but he had no better success; she would not or could not speak to him. Thursday morning she saw Amos Wickliff. She seemed brighter, and gave Amos, in the presence of the nurse, the notes and mortgages that she desired released. Thursday evening, about eight o'clock, Amos returned to report how he had done his commissions. He found the house flaming from roof-tree to sills! There was no question of his saving the sick woman. Even as he panted up the hill-side the roof fell in with a crash. Amos screamed to the crowd: "Where is she? Did you save her?" And the Irish char-woman's wail answered him: "I wint in—I wint in whin it was all afire, and the fire jumped at me, so I run; me eyebrows is gone, and I didn't see a sign of her!" Then Amos betook himself to Mrs. Raker, whom he found only after much searching; nor did her story reassure him. She was violently agitated between pity and shock, but, as usual, she kept her head on her shoulders and her wits on duty. She was not in the house when the catastrophe had happened. Allerton had come to see his aunt. He told the nurse that she might go to her sister, her sister's child being ill, and that he would stay with his aunt. Wickliff was expected every moment. And the patient had added her word, "Do go, Mrs. Raker; it's only a step; and take a jar of my plum jelly to Sammy to take his medicine in!" So Mrs. Raker went. She saw the fire first, and that not half an hour from the time she left the house. She saw it flickering in the lower windows. It was she sent her brother-in-law to give the alarm, while she ran swiftly to the house. The whole lower story was ablaze when she got up the hill. To enter was impossible. But Mrs.

O'Shea, the char-woman, and she did find a ladder, and put it against the wall and the window
of Miss Clark's chamber, which window was wide
open, and Mrs. Baker held the ladder while Mrs.
O'Shea, who was of an agile and slimmer build,
clambered up the rounds to look through the
smoke, already mixed with flame. And the room
was empty. Amos at once had the neighborhood
searched, hoping that Allerton had conveyed his
aunt to a place of safety. There was no trace of
either aunt or nephew. But Amos found a boy
who confessed (after some pressure) that he had
been in Miss Margaret's yard, in the vineyard
facing her room. He had been startled by a
kind of rattling noise and a scream. Involuntarily he cowered behind the vines and peered
through at the house. The windows of Miss
Clark's room were closed, or maybe one was open
very slightly; but suddenly this window was
pushed up and Allerton leaned out. He knew
it was Allerton by the square shoulders. He did
not say anything, only turned his head, looking
every way. The boy thought it time to run.
He was clear of the yard and beginning to de-
scend the bluff, when he looked back and saw
Allerton running very swiftly through the circle
of light cast by the electric lamp. All the reporters examined the lad, but he never altered

his tale. " Mr. Allerton looked frightened—he looked awful frightened," he said.

Amos was on the point of sending to the police, when Allerton himself appeared. The incredible story which he told only thickened the suspicions beginning to gather about him.

He said that he had found his aunt disinclined to talk. She told him to go into the other room, for she wished to go to sleep ; and although he had matters of serious import to discuss with her, he could not force his presence on a lady, and he obeyed her. He went into the adjoining room, and there he sat in a chair before the door. The door was the sole means of exit from the bedchamber. The two rooms opened into each other by the door ; and the second room, in which Allerton sat, had a door into a small hall, from which the staircase led down-stairs. Allerton was ready to swear to his story, which was that he had sat in the chair before the door until he heard a singular muffled scream from the other room. Instantly he sprang up, opened the door, and ran into the other room. The bed was opposite the door. To his terror and amazement, the bed was empty, the room was empty. He ran frantically round the room, and then flung up the window, looking out ; but there was nothing to be seen. Moreover, the room was twenty

feet from the ground, nor was there so much as
a vine or a lightning-rod to help a climber.   It
was past believing that a decrepit old woman,
who could not turn in bed alone, should have
climbed out of a window and dropped twenty
feet to the ground.   Besides, there was the boy
watching that side of the house all the time.   He
had seen nothing.   But where was Margaret
Clark ?   The chief of police took the respon-
sibility of arresting Allerton.   Perhaps he was
swayed to this decisive step by the boy's testimony being in a measure corroborated by a
woman of unimpeachable character living in the
neighborhood, who had heard screams, as of something in mortal pain or fear, at about the time
mentioned by the boy.   She looked up to the
house and was half minded to climb the steps ;
but the sounds ceased, the peaceful lights in the
house on the hill were not disturbed, and, chid-
ing her own ears, she passed on.

The fire broke out a little later, hardly a quar-
ter of an hour after Allerton went away.   This
was established by the fact that the boy, who
ran at the top of his speed, had barely reached
home before he heard the alarm - bells.   The
flames seemed to envelop the whole struct-
ure in a flash, which was not so much a matter of marvel as other things, since the house

was of wood, and dry as tinder from a long drought.

It was possible that Allerton was lying, and that while he and the boy were gone the old woman had discovered the fire and painfully crawled down-stairs and out of the burning house; but, in that case, where was she? How could a feeble old woman thus vanish off the face of the earth? The next day the police explored the ruins. They half expected to find the bones of the unfortunate creature. They did not find a shred of anything that resembled bones. If Allerton had murdered his aunt, he had so contrived his crime as to destroy every vestige of the body; and granting him a motive to do such an atrocious deed, why should so venturesome and ingenious a murderer jeopard everything by a wild fairy tale? The reporters found themselves before a blank wall.

"Maybe it *ain't* a fairy tale," Amos Wickliff suggested one day, two days after the mystery. He was giving "the boys" a kind word on the court-house steps.

"It's to be hoped it is a true story," said the youngest and naturally most hardened reporter, "since then he'll die with a better conscience!"

"They never can convict him on the evi-

12

dence," interrupted another man. "I don't
see how they can even hold him."

"That's why folks are mad," said the youngest reporter, with a pitying smile.

"There's something in the talk, then?" said
Amos, shifting his cigar to the other side of his
mouth.

"*Are* they going to lynch that feller?" asked
another reporter.

"Say so," the first young man remarked,
placidly; "a lot of the old lady's chums are
howling about stringing him up. They've the
notion that she was burned alive, and they're
hot over it."

"That's *your* paper, old man; you had 'most
two columns, and made it out Mrs. Kerby heard
squealing *after* the boy did; and pictured the
horrible situation of the poor old helpless woman
writhing in anguish, and the fire eating nearer
and nearer. Great Scott! it made *me* crawl to
read it; and I saw a crowd down-town in the
park, and if one fellow wasn't reading your
blasted blood-curdler out loud; and one woman
was crying and telling about the old party lend-
ing her money to buy her husband's coffin, and
then letting her off paying. That made the
crowd rabid. At every sentence they let off a
howl. You needn't be grinning like a wild-cat;

it ain't funny to that feller in jail, I bet. Is it, Amos ?"

"You boys better call off your dogs, if you can get 'em," was all the sheriff deigned to answer, and he rose as he spoke. He did not look disturbed, but his placid mask belied him. Better than most men he knew what stormy petrels "the newspaper boys" were. And better than any man he knew what an eggshell was his jail. "I'd almost like to have 'em bust that fool door, though," he grimly reflected, "just to show the supervisors I knew what I was talking about. I'll get a new jail out of those old roosters, or they'll have to get a new sheriff. But meanwhile—" He fell into a perplexed and gloomy reverie, through which his five years' acquaintance with the lost woman drifted pensively, as a moving car will pass, slowly revealing first one familiar face and then another. "I suppose I'm what the lawyers would call her next friend — hereabouts, anyhow," he mused, "and yet you might say it was quite by accident we started in to know each other, poor old lady !" The cause of the first acquaintance was as simple as a starved cat which a jury of small boys were preparing to hang just under the bluff. Amos cut down the cat, and almost in the same rhythm, as the disciples of Delsarte would say, cuffed the nearest executioner, while the others fled. Amos hated cats, but this one, as if recognizing his good-will (and perhaps finding some sweet drop in the bitter existence of peril and starvation that he knew, and therefore loath to yield it), clung to Amos's knees and essayed a feeble purr of gratitude. Well, pussy," said Amos, "good-bye!" But the cat did not stir, except to rub feebly again. It was a black cat, very large, ghastly thin, with the rough coat of neglect, and a pair of burning eyes that might have reminded Amos of Poe's ghastly conceit were he not protected against such fancies by the best of protectors. He could not remember disagreeably that which he had never read. "Pussy, you're about starved," said Amos. "I believe I've got to give you a stomachful before I turn you loose."

"*I'll* give the kitty something to eat," said a voice in the air.

Amos stared at the clouds; then he whirled on his heel and recognized both the voice, which had a different accent and quality of tone from the voices that he was used to hear, and the little, shabby, gray-headed woman who was scrambling down to him.

"*Will* you?" exclaimed Amos, in relief, for he knew her by repute, although they had never

"'ILL GIVE THE KITTY SOMETHING TO EAT'"

looked each other in the face before. "Well, that's very nice of you, Miss Clark."

"I'll keep him with pleasure, sir," said the old woman. "I've had a bereavement lately. My cat died. She was 'most at the allotted term, I expect, but so spry and so intelligent I couldn't realize it. I couldn't somehow feel myself attracted to any other cat. But this poor fugitive— Come here, sir !"

To Amos's surprise, the cat summoned all its forces and, after one futile stagger, leaped into her arms. A strange little shape she looked to him, as she stood, with her head too large for her emaciated little body, which was arrayed in a coarse black serge suit, plainly flotsam and jetsam of the bargain counter, planned for a woman of larger frame. Yet uncouth as the woman looked, she was perfectly neat.

"I'm obliged to you for saving the poor creature," she said.

"I'm obliged to you, ma'am, for taking it off my hands," said Amos. He bowed; she returned his bow—not at all in the manner or with the carriage to be expected of such a plain and ill-clad presence. Amos considered the incident concluded. But a few days later she stopped him on the street, nervously smiling. "That cat, sir," she began in her abrupt way—she never seemed to open a conversation ; she dived into it with a shiver, as a timid swimmer plunges into the water—"that cat," said she, "that cat, sir, is a right intelligent animal, and he has pleased the Colonel. He's so fastidious I was afraid, though I didn't mention it ; but they are very congenial."

"I'm glad they're friendly," says Amos ; "the Colonel would make mince-meat of an uncongenial cat. What do you call the cat ?"

"I couldn't, on account of circumstances, you know, call him after my last cat, Miss Margaret Clark, so I call him Esquire Clark. He knows his name already. I thank you again, sir, for saving him. I just stopped you so as to tell you I had a lot of ripe gooseberries I'd be glad to have you send and pick."

"Why, that's good of you," said Amos. "I guess the boys at the jail would like a little gooseberry sauce."

She nodded and turned round ; the words came over her shoulder : "Say, sir, I expect you wouldn't give them jam ? It's a great deal better than sauce, and—I don't mind letting you have the extra sugar." Amos was more bewildered than he showed, but he thanked her, and did, in fact, come that afternoon with a buggy. The first object to greet him was the

large white head and the large black jaws of the
Colonel, chained to a post. Amos, who is the
friend of all dogs, and sometimes has an un-
invited following of stray curs, gave the snarling
figure-head a nod and a careless greeting : "All
right, young feller. Don't disturb yourself. I'm
here, all proper and legal. How are you ?" The
redoubtable Colonel began to wag his tail ; and
as Amos came up to him he actually fawned on
him with manifestations of pleasure.

"I guess he's safe to unloose, ma'am," said
Amos.

Old Twentypercent was looking on with a
strange expression. "He likes you, sir ; I never
saw him like a stranger before."

"Well, most dogs like me," said Amos. "I
guess they understand I like them."

"I reckon you're a good man," said Old
Twentypercent, solemnly. From this auspicious
beginning the acquaintance slowly but steadily
waxed into a queer kind of semi - friendship.
Amos always bowed to the old woman when he
met her on the street. She sent the prisoners in
the jail fruit every Sunday during the season ;
and Amos, not to be churlish, returned the
courtesy with a flowering plant, now and then,
in winter. But he never carried his gifts himself, esteeming that such conduct would be an

intrusion on a lady who preferred a retired life. Esquire Clark, however, was of a social turn. He visited the jail often. The first time he came Amos sent him back. The messenger, Mrs. Raker, was received at the door, thanked warmly, sent away loaded with fruit and flowers, but not asked over the threshold, which made Amos the surer that he was right in not going himself. Nevertheless, he did go to see Miss Clark, but hardly on his own errand. A carpenter in the town, a good sort of thriftless though industrious creature, came to Amos to borrow some money. He explained that he needed it to pay interest on a debt, and that his tools were pledged for security. The interest, he mourned, was high, and the debt of long standing. The creditor was Old Twentypercent.

"It's a shame I 'ain't paid it off before, and that's a fact," he concluded; "but a feller with nine children can't pay nothing—not even the debt of nature—for he's 'fraid to die and leave them. And the blamed thing's been a-runnin' and a-runnin', like a ringworm, and a-eatin' me up. Though my wife she says we've more'n paid her up in interest." Amos had an old kindness for the man, and after a visit to his wife—he holding the youngest two of the nine (twins) on his knees and keeping the peace with candy—he told the pair he would ask Miss Clark to allow a third extension, on the payment of the interest.

"Well, but I don't know's he's even got that," said the wife, anxiously. "We'd a lot of expenses; I don't s'pose we'd orter had the twins' photographs taken this month, but they was so delicate I was 'fraid we wouldn't raise 'em; and Mamie really couldn't go to school without new shoes. Children's a blessing, I s'pose, but it's a blessing poor folks had got to pay for in advance!"

"*So!*" says Amos. "Well, we'll have to see to that much, I guess. I'll go this night." He betook himself to his errand in a frame of mind only half distasteful. The other half was curious. His visit fell on a summer night, a Sunday night, when the air was soft and still and sweet with the tiny hum of insects and the smell of drying grass and the mellow resonance of the church-bells. Amos climbed the clay stairs. The white porcupine blazed above the bluffs. It gave light enough to see the color of the grass and flowers; yet not a real color, only the ghost of scarlet and green and white, and only a ghost of the violet sky, while all about the devouring shadows sank form and color alike in their olive blacks. The stars were out in the sky and the south wind in the trees. Amos stepped across the lawn—he

was a light walker although a heavy - weight—
and stopped before the front door, which had
long windows on either side. He had his arm
outstretched to knock ; but he did not knock .
he stood and watched the green holland shade
that screened the window rise gradually. He
could see the room, a large room, uncarpeted,
whereby the steps of the inmate echoed on the
boards. He could see a writing - desk, a table,
and four or five chairs. These chairs were entirely different from anything else in the room ;
they were of pretty shape and extremely comfortable. Immediately the curtain descended at
a run, and the old woman's voice called, '' You're
a *bad* cat ; don't you do that again !'' The voice
went on, as if to some one present : '' Did you
ever see such a trying beast ? Why, he's almost
human ! Now, you watch ; the minute I turn
away from that window, that cat will pull up the
shade.'' It appeared that she was right, for the
curtain instantly rolled up again. '' No, honey,''
said Miss Clark, '' you mustn't encourage the
kitty to be naughty. 'Squire, if I let that curtain stay a minute, will you behave !'' A dog's
growl emphasized this gentle reproof. '' You
see the Colonel disapproves. Don't pull the
dog's tail, honey. Oh, mercy ! *'Squire !''* Amos
heard a crash, and in an instant a flame shot up

in a cone; and he, with one blow dislodging the screen from the open window, plunged into the smoke. The cat had tipped over the lamp, and the table was in a blaze. Amos's quick eye caught sight of the box which served Esquire for a bed. He huddled feather pillow and rug on the floor to invert the box over the blaze. The fire was out in a moment, and Margaret had brought another lamp from the kitchen. Then Amos had leisure to look about him. There was no one in the room. Yet that was not the most pungent matter for thought. Old Margaret, whom he had considered one of the plainest women in the world, as devoid of taste as of beauty, was standing before him in a black silk gown. A fine black silk, he pronounced it. She had soft lace about her withered throat, and a cap with pink ribbons on her gray hair, which looked silvery soft. Her skin, too, seemed fairer and finer : and there were rings that flashed and glowed on her thin fingers. It was not Old Twentypercent; it was a stately little gentlewoman that stood before him. " How did you happen to come, sir ?"—she spoke with coldness.

"I came on an errand, and I was just at the door when the curtain flew up and the cat jumped across the table."

She involuntarily caught her breath, like one relieved ; then she smiled. "You mustn't be too hard on 'Squire ; he's of a nervous temperament; I think he sees things—things outside our ken."

Meanwhile Amos was unable not to see that there had been on the table a tumbler full of some kind of shrub, four glasses, and a decanter of wine. And there had been wine in all the glasses. But where were the drinkers ? There were four or five plates on the table, and a segment of plum-cake was trodden underfoot on the floor. Before she did anything else, old Margaret carefully, almost scrupulously, gathered up the crumbs and carried them away. When she returned she carried a plate of cake and a glass of wine. This refreshment was proffered to Amos.

"It's a domestic port," she said, "but well recommended. I should be right glad to have you sit down and have a glass of wine with me, Mr. Sheriff."

"Perhaps you mayn't be so glad when you hear my errand," said Amos.

She went white in a second, and her fingers curved inward like the fingers of the dying ; she was opening and shutting her mouth without making a sound. He had seen a man hanged

once, and that face had worn the same ghastly
stare of expectation.

"If you knew I was come to beg off one of
your debtors, for instance," he went on ; "that's
my errand, if you want to know."

Her face changed. "It will go better after a
glass of wine," said she, again proffering the wine
by a gesture—she didn't trust her hand to pass
the tray.

Amos was a little undecided as to the proper
formula to be used, never having taken wine with
a lady before ; he felt that the usual salutations
among "the boys," such as "Here's how !" or
"Happy days !" or "Well, better luck next
time !" savored of levity if not disrespect ; so
he grew a little red, and the best he could do
was to mumble, "Here's my respects to you,
madam !" in a serious tone, with a bow.

But old Margaret smiled. "It's a long while,"
said she, "since I have taken wine with a — a
gentleman outside my own kin."

"Is that so ?" Amos murmured, politely.
"Well, it's the first time I have had that pleasure with a lady." He was conscious that he was
pleasing her, and that she was smiling about
her, for all the world (he said to himself) as if
she were exchanging glances with some one. A
new idea came to him, and he looked at her

compassionately while he ate his cake, breaking off bits and eating it delicately, exactly as she ate.

She offered him no explanation for the wine-glasses or for the conversation that he had over-heard. He did not hear a sound of any other life in the house than their own. The doors were open, and he could see into the bedroom on one side and into the kitchen on the other. She had lighted another lamp, enabling him to distinguish every object in the kitchen. There was not a carpet in the house, and it seemed impossible that any one could be concealed so quickly without making a sound.

Amos shook his head solemnly. " Poor lady!" said he.

But she, now her mysterious fright was passed, had rallied her spirits. Of her own motion she introduced the subject of his errand. " You spoke of a debtor ; what's the man's name ?"

Amos gave her the truth of the tale, and with some humor described the twins.

" Well, I reckon he has more than paid it," she said at the end. " What do you want ? Were you going to lend him the money ?"

" Well, only the interest money ; he's a good fellow, and he has nine children."

" Who have to be paid for in advance ?" She actually tittered a feeble, surprised little laugh, as she rose up and stepped (on her toes, in the prim manner once taught young gentlewomen) across the room to the desk. She came back with a red-lined paper in her meagre, blue-veined hand. She handed the paper to Amos. "That is a present to you."

"Not the whole note?"

"Yes, sir. Because you asked me. You tell Foley that. And if he's got a dog or a cat or a horse, you tell him to be good to it."

This had been a year ago; and Amos was sure that Foley's gratitude would take the form of a clamor for revenge. Mrs. Foley dated their present prosperity entirely from that day; she had superadded a personal attachment to an impersonal gratitude; she sold Miss Clark eggs, and little Mamie had the reversion of the usurer's shoes. Amos sighed. "Well, I can't blame 'em," he muttered. From that day had dated his own closer acquaintance.

He now occasionally paid a visit at the old gentlewoman's home. Once she asked him to tea. And Raker went about for days in a broad grin at the image of Amos, who, indeed, made a very careful toilet with his new blue sack-coat, white duck trousers, and tan-colored shoes. He told Raker that he had had a delightful supper. Mrs. O'Shea, the char-woman, was without at the kitchen stove, and little Mamie Foley brought in the hot waffles and jam. Esquire Clark showed his gifts by vaulting over the grape-arbor, trying to enter through the wire screen, bent on joining the company, and the Colonel wept audibly outside, until Amos begged for their admission. Safely on their respective seats, their behavior, in general, was beyond criticism. Only once the Colonel, feeling that the frying chicken was unconscionably long in coming his way, gave a low howl of irrepressible feeling ; and Esquire Clark (no doubt from sympathy) leaped after Mamie and the dish.

"'Squire, I'm ashamed of you!" cried Miss Clark ; "Archie, *you* know better!" Amos paid no visible attention to the change of name; but she must have noticed her own slip, for she said: "I never told you the Colonel's whole name, did I? It's Colonel Archibald Cary. I'd like you never to mention it, though. And 'Squire Clark is named after an uncle of mine who raised me, for my parents died when I was a little girl. Clark Byng was his name, and I called the cat by the first part of it."

Amos did not know whether interest would be considered impertinent, so he contented himself with remarking that they were "both pretty names."

"Uncle was a good man," said Miss Clark. "He was only five feet four in height, but very fond of muscular games, and a great admirer of tall men. Colonel Cary was six feet two. I reckon that's about your height?"

"Exactly, ma'am," said Amos.

She sighed slightly; then turned the conversation to Amos's own affairs.

An instinct of delicacy kept him from ever questioning her, and she vouchsafed him no information. Once she asked him to come and see her when he wanted anything that she could give him. "I'm at home to you every day, except the third of the month," said she. On reflection Amos remembered that it was on the third that he had paid his first visit to Miss Clark.

"Well, ma," he remarked, walking up and down in front of his mother's portrait in his office, as his habit was, "it is a queer case, ain't it? But I'm not employed to run the poor old lady to cover, and I sha'n't let any one else if I can help it."

Had Amos been vain, he would have remarked the change in his singular friend since their friendship had begun. Old Margaret wore the decent black gown and bonnet becoming an elderly gentlewoman. She carried a silk umbrella. The neighbors began to address her as

13

"Miss Clark." Amos, however, was not vain, and all he told his mother's picture was that the old lady was quality, and no mistake.

By this time, on divers occasions, she had spoken to Amos of her South Carolina home. Once she told him (in a few words, and her voice was quiet, but her hands trembled) of the yellow-fever time on the lonely plantation in the pine woods, and how in one week her uncle, her brother and his wife, and her little niece had died, and she with her own hands had helped to bury them. "It was no wonder I didn't see things all right after that," she said. Another time she showed him a locket containing the old-fashioned yellow photograph of a man in a soldier's uniform. "He was considered very handsome," said she. Amos found it a handsome face. He would have found it so under the appeal of those piteous eyes had it been as ugly as the Colonel's. "He was killed in the war," she said ; "shot while he was on a visit to us to see my sister. He ran out of the house, and the Yan—your soldiers shot him. It was the fortune of war. I have no right to blame them. But if he hadn't visited our fatal roof he might be living now ; for it was in the very last year of the war. I saw it. I fell down as if shot myself—better if I had been."

"Well, I call that awful hard," said Amos ; " I should think you would have gone crazy !"

"Oh no, sir, no !" she interrupted, eagerly. " My mind was perfectly clear."

"But how you must have suffered !"

" Yes, I suffered," said she. " I never thought to speak of it."

A week after this conversation her nephew came. The day was September 3d. Nevertheless, on that Wednesday night she summoned Amos. He had been out in the country ; but Mrs. Raker had heard through little Minnie Foley, who came for some crab-apples and found Miss Clark moaning on the cellar floor. The jail being but a few blocks away, Mrs. Raker was on the scene almost as soon as George Washington. By the time Amos arrived the two doctors had gone and Miss Clark was in bed, and the white bedspread or white pillows under her head were hardly whiter than her face.

"Mrs. Raker's making some gruel," said she, feebly, "and if you'll stay here I have something to say. It's an odd thing, you'll think," she added, wistfully, when he was in the armchair by her bed (it was one of the chairs from the other room, he noticed)—"an odd thing for a miserable old woman with no kin and no friends to be loath to leave ; but I'm like a cat, I reckon.

It near tore my soul up by the roots to leave the old place, and now it's as bad here."

"Don't you talk such nonsense as leaving, Miss Clark," Amos tried to console her. But she shook her head. And Amos, recalling what the doctors said, felt his words of denial slipping back into his throat. He essayed another tack. "Don't you talk of having no friends here either. Why, poor Mrs. O'Shea has blued all my shirts that she was washing, so they're a sight to see— all for grief; and little Mamie Foley ran crying all the way down the street."

"The poor child!"

"And why are you leaving *me* out?"

"I don't want to leave you out, Mr. Sheriff—"

"Oh, say Amos when you're sick, Miss Clark," he cried, impulsively; she seemed so little, so feeble, and so alone.

"You're a kind man, Amos Wickliff," said she. "Now first tell me, would you give the Colonel and 'Squire a home as long as they need it?"

Amos gave an inward gasp; but it may be imputed to him for righteousness some day that there was only an imperceptible pause before he answered, "Yes, ma'am, I will; and take good care of them, too."

"Here's something for you, then; take it

now." She handed him a large envelope, sealed. "It's for any expenses, you know. And—I'll send 'em over to-morrow."

He took the package rather awkwardly. "Now you know you have a nephew—" he began.

"I know, and I know why he's here, too. And in that paper is my will; but don't you open it till I'm dead a month, will you?"

Amos promised in spite of a secret misgiving.

"And now," she went on, in her nervous way, "I want you to do something right kind for me— not now—when Mrs. Raker goes; she's a good soul, and I hope you'll give her the envelope I've marked for her. Yes, sir, I want you to do something for me when she's gone. Move in the four chairs from down-stairs—the pretty ones —all the rest are plain, so you can tell; and fetch me the tray with the wineglasses and the bottle of shrub—you'll find the tray in the buffet with the red curtains down-stairs in my office. Then you go into the kitchen—I feel so sorry to have to ask a gentleman to do such things, but I do want them—and you'll see a round brown box with Cake marked on it in curly gilt letters, and you'll find a frosted cake in there wrapped up in tissue-paper; and you take it out, and get a knife out of the drawer, and fetch all those things up to me. And then, Amos Wickliff, all

the friend I've got in the world, you go and stay
outside—it ain't cold or I wouldn't ask it of you
—you stay until you hear my bell.   Will you ?"

Amos took the thin hand, involuntarily outstretched, and patted it soothingly between both
his strong brown hands.

" Of course I will," he promised.   And after
Mrs. Raker's departure he did her bidding, saying often to himself, " Poor lady!"

When the bell rang, and he came back, the
wineglasses and the decanter were empty, and
the cake was half gone.   He made no comment,
she gave him no explanation.   Until Mrs. Raker
returned she talked about releasing some of her
debtors.

The following morning he came again.

" I declare," thought Amos, " when I think of
that morning, and how much brighter she looked,
it makes me sick to think of her as dead.   She
had been doing a lot of things on the sly, helping folks.   It was her has been sending the
money for the jail dinner on Christmas, and the
ice-cream on the Fourth, and books, too.   'It's
so terrible to be a prisoner,' says she.   Wonder,
didn't she know?   I declare I *hate* her to be dead!
Ain't it possible—Lord! wouldn't that be a go?"
He did not express even to himself his sudden
flash of light on the mystery.   But he went his

ways to the armory of the militia company, the office of the chief of police (which was the very next building), and to the fire department. At one of these places he wrote out an advertisement, which the reporters read in the evening papers, and found so exciting that they all flocked together to discuss it.

All this did not take an hour's time. It was to be observed that at every place which he visited he first stepped to the telephone and called up the jail. "Are you all right there, Raker?" he asked. Then he told where he was going. "If you need, you can telephone me there," he said.

"I guess Amos isn't taking any chances on this," the youngest reporter, who encountered him on his way, remarked to the chief of police.

The chief replied that Amos was a careful man ; he wished some others would be as careful, and as sure they were right before they went ahead ; a good deal of trouble would be avoided.

"That's right," said the reporter, blithely, and went his lightsome way, while the chief scowled.

Amos returned to the jail. He found the street clear, but little knots of men were gathering and then dispersing in the street facing the jail. Amos thought that he saw Foley's face in the crowd, but it vanished as he tried to distinguish it. "No doubt he's egging them on," muttered Amos. He was rather taken aback when Raker (to whom he offered his suspicions) assured him, on ear evidence, that Foley was preaching peace and obedience to the law. "He's an Irishman, too," muttered Amos; "that's awful queer." He spent a long time in a grim reverie, out of which he roused himself to despatch a boy for the evening papers. "And you mark that advertisement, and take half a dozen copies to Foley"—thus ran his directions—"tell him I sent them; and if he knows anybody would like to read that 'ad,' to send a paper to *them*. Understand?"

"Maybe it's a prowl after a will-o'-wisp," Amos sighed, after the boy was gone, "but it's worth a try. Now for our young man!"

Allerton was sitting in his cell, in an attitude of dejection that would have been a grateful sight to the crowd outside. He was a slim-waisted, broad - shouldered, gentle - mannered young fellow, whose dark eyes were very bright, and whose dark hair was curly, and longer than hair is usually worn by Northerners not studying football at the universities. He had a mildly Roman profile and a frank smile. His clothes seemed almost shabby to Amos, who never grudged a dollar of his tailor's bills; but the

little Southern village whence he came was used
to admire that glossy linen and that short-skirt-
ed black frock-coat.

At Amos's greeting he ran forward excitedly.
"Are they coming?" he cried. "Say, sheriff,
you'll give me back my pistol if they come; you'll
give me a show for my life?"

Amos shrugged his shoulders impatiently.
"Your life's all right," said he; "it's how to
keep from hurting the other fellows I'm after.
The fire department will turn out and sozzle 'em
well, and if that won't do they will have to face
the soldiers; but I hope to the Lord your aunt
won't let it come to that."

"Do you think my aunt is living?"

"I don't see how she could be burned up so
completely. But see here, Mr. Allerton, wasn't
there no trap-door in the room?"

"No, sir; there was no carpet on the floor; she
hadn't a carpet in the house. Besides, how could
she, sick as she was, get down through a trap-
door and shut it after her? And you could *see*
the boards, and there was no opening in them."

"So Mrs. O'Shea says, too," mused the sheriff;
"but let's go back. Had your aunt any motive
for trying to escape you?"

"I'm afraid she thought she had," said the
young man, gravely.

"Mind telling me ?"

"No, sir. I reckon you don't know my aunt was crazy ?"

"I've had some such notion. She lost her mind when they all died of yellow-fever—or was it when Colonel Cary was killed ?"

"I don't know precisely. I imagine that she was queer after his death, and all the family dying later, that finished the wreck. There were some painful circumstances connected with the colonel's death—"

"I've heard them."

"Yes, sir. Well, sir, my mother was not to blame—not so much to blame as you may think. She was almost a stranger to her sister, raised in another State ; and she had never seen her or Colonel Cary, her betrothed ; and when she did see him—well, sir, my mother was a beautiful, daring, brilliant girl, and poor Aunt Margaret timid and awkward. *She* broke the engagement, not Cary."

"It was to see your mother he came to the plantation !"

"Yes, sir. And he was killed. Poor Aunt Margaret saw it. She came back to the house riding in a miserable dump - cart, holding his head in her lap. She wouldn't let my mother come near him. ' Now he knows which loved

him best,' she said. 'He's *mine!*' And it didn't
soften her when my mother married my father.
She seemed to think that proved she hadn't
cared for Colonel Cary. Then the yellow-fever
came, and they all went. Her mind broke down
completely then; she used to think that on the
day Colonel Cary was shot they all came back for
a while, and she would set chairs for them and
offer them wine and cake—as if they were visiting her. And after they left she would pour the
wine in the glasses into the grate and burn the
cake. She said that they enjoyed it, and ate
really, but they left a semblance. She got hold
of some queer books, I reckon, for she had the
strangest notions; and she spent no end of money
on some spiritual mediums; greedy harpies that
got a heap of money out of her. My father and
mother had come to Cary Hall, then, to live,
and of course they didn't like it. The great
trouble, my mother often said to me, was that
though they were sisters, they were raised apart,
and were as much strangers as—we are. You
can imagine how they felt to see the property
being squandered. Ten thousand dollars, sir,
went in one year—"

"Are you sure it did go?" said the sheriff.

"Well, the property was sold, and we never
saw anything afterwards of the money. And the

estate wasn't a bottomless well. It isn't so strange, sir, that—that they had poor Aunt Margaret cared for."

"At an insane asylum?"

"Yes, sir, for five years. I confess," said the young man, jumping up and pacing the room—"I confess I think it was a horrible place, horrible. But they didn't know. It was only after she recovered her senses and was released that we began to understand what she suffered. Not so much then, for she was shy of us all. She was so scared, poor thing! And then—we began to suspect that she was not cured of her delusions. Maybe there *were* consultations and talk about her, though indeed, sir, my mother has assured me many times that there was no intention of sending her back. But she is very shrewd, and she would notice how doors would be shut and the conversation would be changed when she entered a room, and her suspicions were aroused. She managed to raise some money on a mortgage, and she ran away, leaving not a trace behind her. My mother has reproached herself ever since. And we've tried to find her. It has preyed upon my mother's mind that she might be living somewhere, poor and lonely and neglected. We are not rich people," said the young man, lifting his head proudly, "but we have enough. I come to offer Aunt Margaret money, not to ask it. We've kept up the place, and bit by bit paid off the mortgage, though it has come hard sometimes. And it was awkward the title being in that kind of shape, and ma wouldn't for a long time get it quieted."

"But how did you ever find out she was *here?*"

The young Southerner smiled. "I reckon I owe being in this scrape at all to your gentlemen of the press. One of them wrote a kind of character-sketch about her, describing her—"

"I know. He's the youngest man on the list, and an awful liar, but he does write a mighty readable story."

"He did this time," said Allerton, dryly; "so readable it was copied in the papers all over, I expect; anyhow, it was copied in our local sheet —inside, where they have the patent insides, you know. It was entitled 'A Usurer, but Merciful!' I showed it to my mother, and she was sure it was Aunt Margaret. Even the name was right, for her whole name is Margaret Clark Cary. She hadn't the heart to cast the name away, and she thought, Clark being a common name, she wouldn't be discovered."

Amos, who had sat down, was nursing his ankle. "Do you suppose," said he, slowly—"do you suppose that taking it to be the case she wasn't so much hurt as the doctors supposed, that *then* she could get out of the room ?"

"I don't see how she could. She was in the room, in the bed, when I went out. I sat down before the door. She couldn't pass me. I heard a screech after a while, a mighty queer sound, and I ran in. Sir, I give you my word of honor, the bed was empty ! the room was empty!"

"How was the room lighted ?"

"By a large lamp with a Rochester burner, and some fancy of hers had made her keep it turned up at full blaze. Oh, you could see every inch of the room at a glance ! And then, too, I ran all round it before I ran to the window, pushed it up, and looked out. I would be willing to take my oath that the room was empty."

"You looked under the bed ?"

"Of course. And in the closet. I tell you, sir, there was no one in the room."

Amos sat for the space of five minutes, it seemed to the young man, really perhaps for a full minute, thinking deeply. Then, "I can't make it out," said he, "but I believe you are telling the truth." He stood up ; the young man also rose. In the silence wherein the younger man tried to formulate something of his gratitude and yet keep his lip from quivering (for he had been sore beset by homesickness and divers ugly fears during the last day), the roar of the crowd without beat through the bars, swelling ominously. And now, all of an instant, the jail was penetrated by a din of its own making. The prisoners lost their heads. They began to scream inquiries, to shriek at each other. Two women whose drunken disorder had gone beyond the station - house restraints, and who were spending a week in jail, burst into deafening wails, partly from fright, partly from pity, and largely from the general craving of their condition to make a noise.

"Never mind," said Amos, laying a kindly hand on young Allerton's shoulder, "the Company B boys are all in the yard. But I guess you will feel easier if you go down-stairs. Parole of honor you won't skip off?"

"Oh, God bless you, sir!" cried Allerton. "I couldn't bear to die this way; it would kill my mother! Yes, yes, of course I give my word. Only let me have a chance to fight, and die fighting—"

"No dying in the case," Amos interrupted; "but what in thunder are the cusses cheering for? Come on; this needs looking into. *Cheering!*"

He hurried down the heavy stairs into the hall, where Raker, a little paler, and Mrs. Raker, a little more flushed than usual, were examining the bolts of the great door.

Amos flung a glare of scorn at it, and he snorted under his breath : "Locks ! No need of locking *You!* I could bust you with the hose !"

As if in answer, the cheering burst forth anew, and now it was coupled with his name : "Wickliff ! Amos ! *Amos!*"

"Let me out!" commanded Wickliff, and he slipped back the bolts. He stepped under the light of the door-lamp outside, tall and strong, and cool as if he had a Gatling gun beside him.

A cheer rolled up from the crowd—yes, not only from the crowd, but from the blue-coated ranks massed to one side, and the young faces behind the bayonets.

Amos stared. He looked fiercely from the mob to the guardians of the law. Then, amid a roar of laughter, for the crowd perfectly understood his gesture of bewilderment and anger, Foley's voice bellowed, "All right, sheriff; we've got her safe !"

They tell to this day how the iron sheriff, whose composure had been proof against every test brought against it, and whom no man had ever before seen to quail, actually staggered

against the door. Then he gave them a broad
grin of his own, and shouted with the rest, for
there in the heart of the rush jailward, lifted
up on a chair—loaned, as afterwards appeared
(when it came to the time for returning), from
Hans Obermann's "Place"—sat enthroned old
Margaret Clark ; and she was looking as if she
liked it !

They got her to the jail porch ; Amos pacified
the crowd with free beer at Obermann's, and
carried her over the threshold in his arms.

He put her down in the big arm-chair in his
office, opposite the portraits of his parents, and
Esquire Clark slid into the room and purred at
her feet, while Mrs. Raker fanned her. It was
rather a chilly evening, the heat having given
place to cold in the sudden fashion of the climate ; but good Mrs. Raker knew what was due
to a person in a faint or likely to faint, and she
did not permit the weather to disturb her rules.
Calmly she began to fan, saying meanwhile, in a
soothing tone, "There, there, don't *you* worry !
it's all right !"

Raker stood by, waiting for orders and smiling
feebly. And young Allerton simply gasped.

"You were at Foley's, then ?" Amos was the
first to speak—apart from Mrs. Raker's crooning,
which, indeed, was so far automatic that it can

14

hardly be called speech ; it was merely a vocal exercise intended to quiet the mind. "You *were* at Foley's, then ?" says Amos.

"Yes, sir," very calmly ; but her hands were clinching the arms of the chair.

"And you saw my advertisement in this evening paper ?"

"Yes, sir ; Foley read it out to me. You begged M. C. C. to come back and help you because you were in great embarrassment and trouble—and you promised me nobody should harm me."

"No more nobody shall !" returned Amos.

"But maybe you can't help it. Never mind. When I heard about how they were talking about lynching him"—she indicated her nephew—"I felt terrible ; the sin of blood-guiltiness seemed to be resting on my soul ; but I couldn't help it. Mr. Sheriff, you don't know I—I was once in—in an insane asylum. I was !"

"That's all right," said Amos. "I know all about that."

"There, there, there !" murmured Mrs. Raker, "don't think of it !"

"It wasn't that they were cruel to me—they weren't that. They never struck or starved me ; they just gave me awful drugs to keep me quiet ; and they made me sit all day, every day, week

in, week out, month in, month out, on a bench
with other poor creatures, who had enough company in their horrible dreams. If I lifted my
hands there was some one to put them down
to my side and say, in a soft voice, 'Hush, be
quiet!' That was their theory—absolute rest!
They thought I was crazy because I could see
more than they, because I had visitors from the
spirit-land—"

" I know," interrupted Amos. " I was there
one night. But I—"

" You couldn't see them. It was only I. They
came to *me*. It was more than a year after they
all died, and I was so lonely—oh, nobody knows
how desolate and lonely I was!—and then a
medium came. She taught me how to summon
them. At first, though I made all the prepara-
tions, though I put out the whist cards for uncle and Ralph and Sadie, and the toys for little
Ro, I couldn't seem to think they were there;
but I kept on acting as if I knew they were
there, and having faith; and at last they did
come. But they wouldn't come in the asylum,
because the conditions weren't right. So at last
I felt I couldn't bear it any longer. I felt like
I was false to the heavenly vision; but I couldn't
stand it, and so I pretended I didn't see them
and I never had seen them; and whatever they

said I ought to feel I pretended to feel, and I
said how wonderful it was that I should be
cured ; and that made them right pleased ; and
they felt that I was quite a credit to them, and
they wrote my sister that I was cured. I went
home, but only to be suspected again, and so I
ran away. I had put aside money before, thou-
sands of dollars, that they thought that I spent.
They thought I gave a heap of it to that medium and her husband ; I truly only gave them
five hundred dollars. So I went forth. I hid
myself here. I was happy here, where *they*
could come, until—until I saw Archibald Allerton on the street and overheard him inquiring
for me. I was dreadfully upset. But I decided
in a minute to flee again. So I drew some
money out of the bank, and I bought a blue
calico and a sun-bonnet not to look like myself ;
and I went home and wrote that letter I gave
you, Mr. Sheriff, with my will and the money."

"The parcel is unopened still," said Amos.
"I gave you my word, you know."

"Yes, I know. I knew you would keep your
word. And it was just after I wrote you I slipped
down the cellar stairs. It came of being in a
hurry. I made sure I never *would* get on my
feet again, but very soon I discovered that I was
more scared than hurt. And I saw then there

might be a chance of keeping him off his guard if he thought I was like to die, and that thus I might escape the readier. It was not hard to fool the doctors. I did just the same with them I did with the asylum folks. I said yes whenever I thought they expected it, and though I had some contradictory symptoms, they made out a bad state of things with the spine, and gave mighty little hope of my recovery. But what I hadn't counted on was that my *friends* would take such good care of me. I didn't know I had friends. It pleased me so I was wanting to cry for joy ; yet it frightened me so I didn't know which way to turn."

" But, great heavens ! Aunt Margaret," the young Southerner burst out, unable to restrain himself longer, " you had no need to be so afraid of *me !*"

The old woman looked at him, more in suspicion than in hope, but she went on, not answering : " The night I did escape, it was by accident. I never would say one word to him hardly, though he tried again and again to start a talk ; but I would seem too ill ; and he's a Cary, anyhow, and couldn't be rude to a lady. That night he went into the other room. He was so quiet I reckoned he was asleep, and, thinking that here might be a chance for me, I slipped out of bed, soft as soft, and slipped over to the crack of the door—it just wasn't closed!—and I peeked in on him—"

"And you were behind the door when he heard the noise?" exclaimed Amos. "But what made the noise?"

"Oh, I reckon just 'Squire jumping out of the window; he gave a kind of screech."

"But I don't understand," cried Allerton. "I went into the room, and it was empty."

"No, sir," said Miss Cary, plucking up more spirit in the presence of Wickliff—"no, sir; I was behind the door. You didn't push it shut."

"But I ran all round the room."

"No, sir; not till you looked out of the window. While you were looking out of the window I slipped out of the door; and I was so scared lest you should see me that I wasn't afraid of anything else; and I got down-stairs while you were looking in the closet, and found my clothes there, and so got out."

"But I was *sure* I went round the room first," cried Allerton.

"Very likely; but you see you didn't," remarked Amos.

"It was because I remembered stubbing my toe"—Allerton was painfully ploughing up his memories—"I am *certain* I stubbed my toe, and

it must have been going round the—no ; by—
I beg your pardon—I stubbed it against the bed,
going to the window. I was all wrong."

"Just so," agreed Amos, cheerfully. "And
then *you* went to Foley, Miss Cary. Trust an
Irishman for hiding anybody in trouble ! But
how did the house catch fire ? Did you—"

But old Margaret protested vehemently that
here at least she was sackless ; and Mrs. Raker
unexpectedly came to the rescue.

"I guess I can tell that much," said she.
" 'Squire came back, and he's got burns all over
him, and he's cut with glass bad ! I guess he
jumped back into the house and upset a lamp
once too often !"

"I see it all," said Amos. "And then you
came back to rescue your nephew—"

"No, sir," cried Margaret Cary ; "I came
back because they said you were in trouble. It's
wicked, but I couldn't bear the thought he'd
take me back to the crazies. I'm an old woman ;
and when you're old you want to live in a house
of your own, in your own way, and not be
crowded. And it's so awful to be crowded by
crazies ! I couldn't bear it. I said he must take
his chance ; and I wouldn't read the papers for
fear they would shake my resolution. It was
Foley read your advertisement to me. And then

I knew if you were in danger, whatever happened to me, I would have to go."

Amos wheeled round on young Allerton. "Now, young fellow," said he, "speak out. Tell your aunt you won't touch a hair of her head ; and she may have her little invisible family gatherings all she likes."

Allerton, smiling, came forward and took his aunt's trembling hand. "You shall stay here or go home to your sister, who loves you, whichever you choose; and you shall be as safe and free there as here," said he.

And looking into his dark eyes — the Cary eyes—she believed him.

The youngest reporter never heard the details of the Clark mystery, but no doubt he made quite as good a story as if he had known the truth.

THE DEFEAT OF AMOS WICKLIFF

THE DEFEAT OF AMOS WICKLIFF

W HAT'S the matter with Amos?" Mrs.
Smith asked Ruth Graves; "the boy
doesn't seem like himself at all."
Amos, at this speaking, was nearer forty than
thirty; but ever since her own son's death he
had been "her boy" to Edgar's mother. She
looked across at Ruth with a wistful kindling of
her dim eyes. "You — you haven't said anything to Amos to hurt his feelings, Ruth?"

Ruth, busy over her embroidery square, set
her needle in with great nicety, and replied, "I
don't think so, dear." Her color did not turn
nor her features stir, and Mrs. Smith sighed.

After a moment she rose, a little stiffly—she
had aged since Edgar's death—walked over to
Ruth, and lightly stroked the sleek brown head.
"I've a very great—*respect* for Amos," she said.
Then, her eyes filling, she went out of the room;
so she did not see Ruth's head drop lower. Re-

spect? But Ruth herself respected him. No
one, no one so much! But that was all. He
was the best, the bravest man in the world; but
that was all. While poor, weak, faulty Ned—
how she had loved him! Why couldn't she love
a right man? Why did not admiration and respect and gratitude combined give her one throb
of that lovely feeling that Ned's eyes used to
give her before she knew that they were false?
Yet it was not Ned's spectral hand that chilled
her and held her back. Three years had passed
since he died, and before he died she had so
completely ceased to love him that she could
pity him as well as his mother. The scorching
anger was gone with the love. But somehow, in
the immeasurable humiliation and anguish of
that passage, it was as if her whole soul were
burned over, and the very power of loving shriv-
elled up and spoiled. How else could she keep
from loving Amos, who had done everything
(she told herself bitterly) that Ned had missed
doing? And she gravely feared that Amos had
grown to care for her. A hundred trifles betrayed his secret to her who had known the
glamour that imparadises the earth, and never
would know it any more. Mrs. Smith had seen
it also. Ruth remembered the day, nearly a
year ago, that she had looked up (she was sing-

ing at their cabinet organ, singing hymns of a
Sunday evening) and had caught the look, not
on Amos's face, but on the kind old face that
was like her mother's. She understood why,
the next day, Mrs. Smith moved poor Ned's
picture from the parlor to her own chamber,
where there were four photographs of him already.

"And now she is reconciled to what will never happen," thought Ruth, "and is afraid it
won't happen. Poor Mother Smith, it never
will!" She wished, half irritably, that Amos
would let a comfortable situation alone. Of
late, during the month or six weeks past, he had
appeared beset by some hidden trouble. When
he did not reckon that he was observed his
countenance would wear an expression of harsh
melancholy ; and more than once had she caught
his eyes tramping through space after her with
a look that made her recall the lines of Tenny-
son Ned used to quote to her in jest—for she
had never played with him :

> "Right thro' his manful breast darted the pang
> That makes a man, in the sweet face of her
> That he loves most, lonely and miserable."

Then, for a week at a time, he would not come
to the village ; he said he was busy with a mur-

der trial. He was not at their house to-day; it was they who were awaiting his return from the court-house, in his own rooms at the jail, after the most elaborate midday dinner Mrs. Raker could devise. The parlor was less resplendent and far prettier than of yore. Ruth knew that the change had come about through her own suggestions, which the docile Amos was always asking. She knew, too, that she had not looked so young and so dainty for years as she looked in her new brown cloth gown, with the fur trimming near enough a white throat to enhance its soft fairness. Yet she sighed. She wished heartily that they had not come to town. True, they needed the things, and, much to Mother Smith's discomfiture, she had insisted on going to a modest hotel near the jail, instead of to Amos's hospitality; but it was out of the question not to spend one day with him. Ruth began to fear it would be a memorable day.

There were his clothes, for instance; why should he make himself so fine for them, when his every-day suit was better than other people's Sunday best? Ruth took an unconscious delight in Amos's wardrobe. There was a finish about his care of his person and his fine linen and silk and his freshly pressed clothes which she likened to his gentle manner with women and the leisurely, pleasant cadence of his voice, which to her quite mended any breaks in her admiration made by a reckless and unprotected grammar. Although she could not bring herself to marry him, she considered him a man that any girl might be proud to win. Quite the same, his changing his dress put her in a panic. Which was nonsense, since she didn't have any reason to suppose— The cold chills were stepping up her spine to the base of her brain ; *that* was his step in the hall !

He opened the door. He was fresh and pressed from the tailor, he was smooth and perfumed from the barber, and his best opal-and-diamond scarf-pin blazed in a new satin scarf. Certainly his presence was calculated to alarm a young woman afraid of love-making.

Nor did his words reassure her. He said, "Ruth, I don't know if you have noticed that I was worried lately."

"I thought maybe you were bothered about some business," lied Ruth, with the first defensive instinct of woman.

"Yes, that's it; it's about a man sentenced to death."

"Oh !" said Ruth.

"Yes, for killing Johnny Bateman. He's applied for a new trial, and the court has just been heard from.   Raker's gone to find out.   If he can't get the hearing, it's the gallows; and I—"

"Oh, Amos, no! that would be too awful! Not *you!*"

"—I'd rather resign the office, if it wouldn't seem like sneaking.   Ah!"   A rap at the door made Amos leap to his feet.   In the rap, so muffled, so hesitating, sounded the diffidence of the bearer of bad news.   "If *that's* Raker," groaned Amos, "it's all up, for that ain't his style of knock!"

Raker it was, and his face ran his tidings ahead of him.

"They refused a new trial?" said Amos.

"Yes, they have," exploded Raker.   "Oh, damn sech justice!   And he's only got three days before the execution.   And it's *here!*   Oh, ain't it h—?"

"Yes, it is," said Amos, "but you needn't say so here before ladies."   He motioned to the portrait and to Ruth, who had leaned out from her chair, listening with a pale, attentive face.

"Please excuse me, ladies," said Raker, absently; "I'm kinder off my base this morning. You see, Amos, my wife she says if hanging Sol is my duty I've jest got to resign, for she won't live with no hangman.   She's terrible upset."

"It ain't your duty; it's mine," said Amos.

"I guess yóu don't like the job any more'n me," stammered Raker, "and it ain't like Joe Raker sneakin' off this way; but what can I do with my woman? And maybe you, not having any wife—"

"No," said Amos, very slowly, "I haven't got any wife; it's easier for me." Nevertheless, the blood had ebbed from his swarthy cheeks.

"But how did it happen?" said Ruth.

"'Ain't Amos told you?" said Raker, whose burden was visibly lightened—he pitied Amos sincerely, but it is much less distressful to pity one's friends than to need to pity one's self. "Well, this was the way: Sol Joscelyn was a rougher in the steel-works across the river, and he has a sweetheart over here, and he took her to the big Catholic fair, and Johnny was there. Johnny was the biggest policeman on the force and the best-natured, and he had a girl of his own, it came out, so there was no cause for Sol to be jealous. He says now it was his fault, and she says 'twas all hers; but my notion is it was the same old story. Breastpins in a pig's nose ain't in it with a pretty girl without common-sense; and that's Scriptur', Mrs. Raker says. But Sol felt awful bad, and he felt so bad he went out and took a drink. He took a good many drinks, I guess;

15

and not being a drinkin' man he didn't know how to carry it off, and he certainly didn't have any right to go back to the hall in the shape he was in. It was a friendly part in Johnny to take him off and steer him to the ferry. But there was a little bad look about it, though Sol went peaceful at last. Sol says they had got down to Front Street, and it was all friendly and cleared up, and he was terrible ashamed of himself the minnit he got out in the air. He was ahead, he says, crossing the street, when he heard Johnny's little dog yelp like mad, and he turned round— of course he wasn't right nimble, and it was a little while before he found poor Johnny, all doubled up on the sidewalk, stabbed in the jugular vein. He never made a sign. Sol got up and ran after the murderer. The mean part is that two men in a saloon saw Sol just as he got up and ran. Naturally they ran after him and started the hue-and-cry, and Sol was so dazed he didn't explain much. Have I got it straight, Amos?"

"Very straight, Joe. You might put in that the prosecuting attorney, Frank Woods, is on his first term and after laurels; and that, un- luckily, there have been three murders in this locality inside the year, and by hook or crook all three of the men got off with nothing but a few years at Anamosa; and public sentiment, in consequence, is pretty well stirred up, and not so particular about who it hits as hitting *somebody;* and that poor Sol had a chump of a lawyer—and you have the state of things."

"But why are you so sure he wasn't guilty?" said Ruth. The shocked look on her face was fading. She was thinking her own thoughts, not Amos's, Raker decided.

"Partly on account of the dog," said Amos. "First thing Sol said when they took him up was, 'Johnny's dog's hurt too'; and true enough we found him (for I was round) crawling down the street with a stab in him. Now, I says, here's a test right at hand; if the dog was stabbed by this young feller he'll tell of it when he sees him, and I fetched him right up to Sol; but, bless my soul, the dog kinder wagged his tail! And he's taken to Sol from the first. Another thing, they never found the knife that did it; said Sol might have throwed it into the river. Tommy rot!—I mean it ain't likely. Sol wasn't in no condition to throw a knife a block or two!"

"But if not he, who else?" said Ruth.

Amos was at a loss to answer her exactly, and yet in language that he considered suitable "to a nice young lady"; but be managed to convey

to her an idea of the villanous locality where the
unfortunate policeman met his death ; and he told
her that from the first, judging by the character
of the blow (" no American man—a decent man
too, like Sol—would have jabbed a man from
behind that way; that's a Dago blow, with a
Dago knife !"), he had suspected a certain Italian woman, who " boarded " in the house beneath
whose evil walls the man was slain. He suspected
her because Johnny had arrested "a great friend
of hers " who turned out to be " wanted," and in
the end was sent to the penitentiary, and the
woman had sworn revenge. " That's all," said
Amos, " except that when I looked her up, she
had skipped. I have a good man shadowing her,
though, and he has found her."

" And that was what convinced you ?"

" That and the man himself. Suppose we
take a look at him. Then I'll have to go to
Des Moines. I suspected this would come, and
I'm all ready."

So the toilet was for the Governor and not for
her; Ruth took shame to herself for a full
minute while Raker was speaking. Amos's dejection came from a cause worthy of such a man
as he. Perhaps all her fancies. . . .

" That will suit," Raker was saying. " He
has been asking for you. I told him."

"Thank you, Joe," said Amos, gratefully.

"I don't propose to leave *all* the dirty jobs to you," growled Raker. And he added under his breath to Ruth, when Amos had stopped behind to strap a bag, "Amos is going to take it hard."

He led the way, through a stone-flagged hall, where the air wafted the unrefreshing cleanliness of carbolic acid and lime, up a stone and iron staircase worn by what hundreds of lagging feet! past grated windows through which how many feverish eyes had been mocked by the brilliant western sky! past narrow doors and the laughter and oaths of rascaldom in the corridor, into an absolutely silent hall blocked by an iron-barred door. There Raker paused to fit a key in the lock, and on his commonplace, florid features dawned a curious solemnity. Ruth found herself breathing more quickly.

The door swung inward. Ruth's first sensation was a sort of relief, the room looked so little like a cell, with its bright chintz on the bed and the mass of nosegays on the table. A black-and-tan terrier bounded off the bed and gambolled joyously over Amos's feet.

"Here's the sheriff and a lady to see you, Sol," Raker announced.

The prisoner came forward eagerly, holding out his hand. All three shook it. He was a

short, cleanly built man, who held his chin
slightly uplifted as he talked. His reddish-
brown hair was strewn over a high white forehead; its disorder did not tally with the neatness of his Sunday suit, which, they told Ruth
afterwards, he had worn ever since his convic-
tion, although previously he had been particular
to wear his working-clothes. Ruth's eyes were
drawn by an uncanny attraction, stronger than
her will, to the face of a man in such a tremen-
dous situation. His skin was fair and freckled,
and had the prison pallor, face and hands. But
the feature that impressed Ruth was his eyes.
They were of a clear, grayish-blue tint, meeting
the gaze directly, without self-consciousness or
bravado, and innocent as a child's. Such eyes
are not unfrequent among working-men, but the
rest of us have learned to hide behind the glass.
He did not look like a man who knew that he
must die in three days. He was smiling. Looking closer, however, Ruth saw that his eyelids
were red, and she observed that his fingers were
tapping the balls of his thumbs continually.

"I'm real glad to see you," he said. "Won't
you set down? Poker, you let the lady alone"
—addressing the dog. "He's just playful; he
won't bite. Mr. Wickliff lets me have him
here; he was Johnny's dog, and he's company

to me. He likes it. They let him out whenever he wants, you know." 'His eyes for a
second passed the faces before him and lingered
on the bare branches of the maple swaying between his window grating and the sky. Was he
thinking that he would see the trees but once,
on one terrible journey?

Raker blew his nose violently.

"Well, I'm off to Des Moines, Sol," said Amos.

"Yes, sir. And about Elly going? I don't
want her to go to all that expense if it won't do
no good. I want to leave her all the money I
can—"

"You never mind about the money." Amos
took the words off his tongue with friendly gruff-
ness. "But she better wait till we see how I
git along. Maybe there'll be no necessity."

"It's a kinder long journey for a young lady,"
said Joscelyn, anxiously, "and it's so hard getting word of those big folks, and I hate to think
of her having to hang round. Elly's so timid
like, and maybe somebody not being polite to
her—"

"I'll attend to all that, Joscelyn. She shall
go in a Pullman, and everything will be fixed."

"Can you git passes? You are doing a terrible lot of things for me, Mr. Wickliff; and Mr.
Raker too, and his good lady" (with a grateful

glance at Raker, who rocked in the rocking-chair and was lapped 'in gloom). "It does seem like you folks here are awful kind to folks in trouble, and if I ever git out—" He was not equal to the rest of the sentence, but Amos covered his faltering with a brisk—

"That's all right. Say, 'ain't you got some new flowers?"

Joscelyn smiled. "Those are from the boys over to the mill. Ten of them boys was over to see me Sunday, no three knowing the others were coming. I tell you when a man gits into trouble he finds out about his friends. I got awful good friends. The roller sent me that box of cigars. And there's one little feller—he works on the hot-bed, one of them kids—and he walked all the six miles, 'cross the bridge and all, 'cause he didn't have money for the fare. Why he didn't have money, he'd spent it all in boot-jack to- bacco and a rosy apple for me. He's a real nice little boy. If—if things was to go bad with me, would you kinder have an eye on Hughey, Mr. Wickliff?"

Amos rose rather hastily. "Well, I guess I got to go now, Sol."

Ruth noticed that Sol got the sheriff's big hand in both his as he said, "I guess you know how I feel 'bout what you and Mr. Raker—" This

THE FAREWELL

time he could not go on, his mouth twitched, and he brushed the back of his hand across his eyes. Ruth saw that the palm had a great white welt on it, and that the sinews were stiffened, preventing the fingers from opening wide. She spoke then. She held out her own hand.

"I know you didn't do it," said she, very deliberately; "and I'm sure we shall get you free again. Don't stop hoping! Don't you stop one minute!"

"I guess I can't say anything better than that," said Amos. In this fashion they got away.

Amos did not part his lips until they were back in his own parlor, where he spoke. "Did you notice his hand?"

Ruth had noticed it.

"A man who saw the accident that gave him those scars told me about it. It happened two years ago. Sol had his spell at the roll, and he was strolling about, and happened to fetch up at the finishing shears, where a boy was straightening the red-hot iron bars. I don't know exactly how it happened; some way the iron caught on a joint of the bed-plates and jumped at him, red-hot. He didn't get out of the way quick enough. It went right through his leg and curved up, and down he dropped with the iron

in him. Near the femoral artery, they said, too;
and it would have burned the walls of the artery
down, and he would have bled to death in a flash.
Sol Joscelyn saw him. He looked round for
something to take hold of that iron with that
was smoking and charring, but there wasn't anything—the boy's tongs had gone between the
rails when he fell. So he—he took his *hands*
and pulled the red-hot thing out! That's how
both his hands are scarred."

"Oh, the poor fellow!" said Ruth ; "and
think of him *here!*"

Amos shook his head and strode to the window. Then he came back to her, where she
was trying to swallow the pain in the roof of her
mouth. He stretched his great hands in front
of him. "How could I ever look at them again
if they pulled that lever ?" he sobbed—for the
words were a sob ; and immediately he flung
himself back to the window again.

"Amos, I know they won't hang him ; why,
they *can't*. If the Governor could only see him."
Ruth was standing, and her face was flushed.
"Why, Amos, *I* thought maybe he might be
guilty until I saw him ! I know the Governor
won't see him, but if we told him about the poor
fellow, if we tried to make him see him as we
do ?"

Amos drearily shook his head. "The Govern-
or is a just man, Ruth, but he is hard as nuts.
Sentiment won't go down with him. Besides,
he is a great friend of Frank Woods, who has got
his back up and isn't going to let me pull his
prisoner out. Of course he's given *his* side."

"The girl—this Elly? If she were to see the
Governor?"

"I don't know whether she'd do harm or not.
She's a nice little thing, and has stood by Sol
like a lady. But it's a toss up if she wouldn't
break down and lose her head utterly. She
comes to see him as often as she can, always
bringing him some little thing or other; and
she sits and holds his hand and cries — never
seems to say three words. Whenever she runs
up against me she makes a bow and says, 'I'm
very much obliged to you, sir,' and looks scared
to death. *I* don't know who to get to go with
her; her mother keeps a working-man's boarding-house; she's a good soul, but—"

He dropped his head on his hand and seemed
to try to think.

It was strange to Ruth that she should long to
go up to him and touch his smooth black hair,
yet such a crazy fancy did flit through her brain.
When she thought that he was suffering because
of her, she had not been moved; but now that

he was so sorely straitened for a man who was nothing to him more than a human creature, her heart ached to comfort him.

"No," said Amos; "we've got to work the other strings. I've got some pull, and I'll work that; then the newspaper boys have helped me out, and folks are getting sorry for Sol; there wouldn't be any clamor against it, and we've got some evidence. I'm not worth shucks as a talker, but I'll take a talker with me. If there was only somebody to keep her straight—"

"Would you trust me?" said Ruth. "If you will, I'll go with her to-morrow."

Amos's eyes went from his mother's picture to the woman with the pale face and the lustrous eyes beneath it. He felt as stirred by love and reverence and the longing to worship as ever mediæval knight; he wanted to kneel and kiss the hem of her gown; what he did do was to open his mouth, gasp once or twice, and finally say, "Ruth, you—you are as good as they make 'em!"

Amos went, and the instant that he was gone, Ruth, attending to her own scheme of salvation, crossed the river. She entered the office of the steel-works, where the officers gave her full information about the character of Sol Joscelyn.

He was a good fellow and a good workman, always ready to work an extra turn to help a fellow-workman. She went to his landlady, who was Elly's mother, and heard of his sober and blameless life. " And indeed, miss, I know of a certainty he never did git drunk but once before, and that was after his mother's funeral ; and she was bedfast for ten years, and he kep' her like a lady, with a hired girl, he did; and he come home to the dark house, and he couldn't bear it, and went back to the boys, and they, meaning well, but foolish, like boys, told him to forget the grief." Ruth went back to Sol's mill, between heats, to seek Sol's young friend. She found the "real nice little boy" with a huge quid in his cheek, and his fists going before the face of another small lad who had "told the roller lies." He cocked a shrewd and unchildish blue eye at Ruth, and skilfully sent his quid after the flying tale-bearer. " Sol Joscelyn ? Course I know him. He's a friend of mine. Give me coffee outer his pail first day I got here ; lets me take his tongs. I'm goin' to be a rougher too, you bet ; I'm a-learnin'. He's the daisiest rougher, he is. It's *grand* to see him ketch them white-hot bars that's jest a-drippin', and chuck 'em under like they was kindling-wood. He's licked my old man, too, for haulin' me round by the

ear. He ain't my own father, so I didn't inter-
fere. Say, you goin' to see Sol to-night ? You
can give him things, can't you ? I got a mince-
pie for him."

Ruth consented to take the pie, and she did
not know whether to laugh or cry when, examining the crust, she discovered, cunningly stowed
away among the raisins and citron, a tiny file.

When she told Sol, he did not seem surprised.
"He's always a - sending of them," said he;
"most times Mr. Raker finds 'em, but once he
got one inside a cigar, and I bit my teeth on it.
He thinks if he can jest git a *file* to me it's all
right. I s'pose he reads sech things in books."

Amos went to Des Moines of a Monday afternoon ; Tuesday night he walked through the jail
gate with his head down, as no one had ever seen
the sheriff walk before.   He kept his eye on the
sodden, frozen grass and the ice-varnished bricks
of the walk, which glittered under the electric
lights ; it was cruelty enough to have to hear
that dizzy ring of hammers ; he would not see ;
but all at once he recoiled and stepped *over* the
sharp black shadow of a beam.   But he had his
composure ready for Raker.

"Well !—he wouldn't listen to you ?"

"No ; he listened, but I couldn't move him,

nor Dennison couldn't, either.   He's honest
about it; he thinks Sol is guilty, and an example
is needed.   Finally I told him I would resign
rather than hang an innocent man.   He said
Woods had another man ready."

"That will be a blow to Sol.   I told him you
would attend to everything.   He said he'd risk
another man if it would make you feel bad—"

"*I* won't risk another man, then.   But the
Governor called my bluff.   Where's Miss Graves?"

"Gone to Des Moines with Elly.   Went next
train after your telegram."

"And Mrs. Smith?"

"She's in reading the Bible to Sol.   I don't
know whether it's doing him any good or not; he
says ' Yes, ma'am,' and ' That's right ' to every
question she asks him ; but I guess some of it's
politeness.   And he seems kinder flighty, and
his mind runs from one thing to another.   But
he says he's still hoping.   He's made a list of all
his things to give away ; and he's said good-bye
to the newspaper boys.   I never supposed that
youngest one had any feeling, but I had to give
him four fingers of whiskey after he come out ;
he was white's the wall, and he hadn't a word to
say.   It's been a terrible day, Amos.   My woman's jest all broke up ; she wanted me to make a
rope-ladder.   Me !   Said she and old Lady Smith

would hide him. 'Polly,' says I, 'I know my
duty; and if I didn't, Amos knows his.' She
'ain't spoke to me since, and we had a picked-up
dinner. Well, *I* can't eat!"

"You best not drink much either, then, Joe,"
said Amos, kindly; and he went his ways. Dark
and painful ways they were that night: but he
never flinched. And the carpenters on the
ghastly machine without the gate (the shadow
of which lay, all night through, on Amos's curtain) said to each other, "The sheriff looks sick,
but he ain't going to take any chances!"

The day came—Sol's last day—and there were
a hundred demands for Amos's decision. In the
morning he made his last stroke for the prisoner. He told Raker about it. "I found the
tool at last," he said, "in the place you suspected. Dago dagger. I've expressed it to Miss
Graves and telegraphed her. It's in *her* hands
now."

"Sol says he 'ain't quit hoping," says Raker.
"Say, the blizzard flag is out; you don't think
you could put it off for weather, being an out-
door thing, you know?"

"No," says Amos, knitting his black brows;
"I know my duty."

Towards night, in one of his many visits to the
condemned man, Sol said, "Elly 'll be sure to

come back from Des Moines in—in time, if she don't succeed, won't she ?"

"Oh, sure," said Amos, cheerfully. He spoke in a louder than common voice when he was with Sol; he fought against an inclination to walk on tiptoe, as he saw Raker and the watch doing. He wished Sol would not keep hold of his hand so long each time they shook hands; but he found his hands going out whenever he entered the room. He had a feeling at his heart as if a string were tightening about it and cutting into it : shaking hands seemed to loosen the string. From Sol, Amos went down-stairs to the telephone to call up the depot. The electricity snapped and roared and buzzed, and baffled his ears, but he made out that the Des Moines train had come in two hours late; the morning train was likely to be later, for a storm was raging and the telegraph lines were down. Elly hadn't come; she couldn't come in time ! Amos changed the call to the telegraph office.

Yes, they had a telegram for him. Just received; been ever since noon getting there. From Des Moines. Read it ?

The sheriff gripped the receiver and flung back his shoulders like a soldier facing the firing-squad. The words penetrated the whir like bullets : "Des Moines, December 8, 189-. Governor refused audience. Has left the city. My sympathy and indignation. T. L. Dennison."

Amos remembered to put the tube up, to ring the bell. He walked out of the office into the parlor ; he was not conscious that he walked on tiptoe or that he moved the arm-chair softly as if to avoid making a noise. He sank back into the great leather depths and stared dully about him. "They've called my bluff !" he whispered ; "there isn't anything left I can do." He could not remember that he had ever been in a similar situation, because, although he had had many a buffet and some hard falls from life, never had he been at the end of his devices or his obstinate courage. But now there was nothing, nothing to be done.

"By-and-by I will go and tell Sol," he thought, in a dull way. No ; he would let him hope a little longer ; the morning would be time enough. . . . He looked down at his own hands, and a shudder contracted the muscles of his neck, and his teeth met.

"Brace up, you coward !" he adjured himself ; but the pith was gone out of his will. That which he had thought, looking at his hands, was that *she* would never want to touch them again. Amos's love was very humble. He knew that Ruth did not love him. Why should she ?

Like all true lovers in the dawn of the New
Day, he was absorbed in his gratitude to her for
the power to love. There is nothing so beautiful, so exciting, so infinitely interesting, as to
love. To be loved is a pale experience beside it,
being, indeed, but the mirror to love, without
which love may never find its beauty, yet holding, of its own right, neither beauty nor charm.
Amos had accepted Ruth's kindness, her sympathy, her goodness, as he accepted the way her
little white teeth shone in her smile, and the
lovely depths of her eyes, and the crisp melody
of her voice—as windfalls of happiness, his by
kind chance or her goodness, not for any merit
of his own. He was grateful, and he did not
presume ; he had only come so far as to wonder
whether he ever would dare— But now he only
asked to be her friend and servant. But to have
her shrink from him, to have his presence odious to her . . . he did not know how to bear
it ! And there was no way out. Not only the
State held him, the wish of the helpless, trusting creature that he had failed to save was
stronger than any law of man. He thought of
Mrs. Raker and her foolish schemes : that woman didn't understand how a man felt. But all
of a sudden he found himself getting up and going quickly to his father's picture ; and he was

saying out loud to the painted soldier : "I know my duty ! I know my duty !" Without, the snow was driving against the window-pane ; that accursed Thing creaked and swayed under the flail of the wind, but kept its stature. Within, the tumult and combat in a human soul was so fierce that only at long intervals did the storm beat its way to his consciousness. Once, stopping his walk, he listened and heard sobs, and a gentle old voice that he knew in a solemn, familiar monotony of tone ; and he was aware that the women were in the other room weeping and praying. And up-stairs Sol, who had never done a mean trick in his life, and been content with so little, and tried to share all he got, was waiting for the sweetheart who never could come, turning that pitiful smile of his to the door every time the wind rattled it, "trying to hope !"

He had not shed a tear for his own misery, but now he leaned his arm on the frame of his mother's portrait and sobbed. He was standing thus when Ruth saw him, when she flashed up to him, cold and wet and radiant.

She was too breathless to speak ; but she did not need to speak.

"You've got it, Ruth !" he cried. "O God, you've got the reprieve !"

"Yes, I have, Amos ; here it is. I couldn't

telegraph because the wires were down, but the Governor and the railroad superintendent fixed it so we could come on an engine. I knew you were suffering. Elly is with Mother Smith and Mrs. Raker, but I—but I wanted to come to you."

If he had thought once of himself he must have heard the new note in her voice. But he did not think once of himself; he could only think of Sol.

"But the Governor, didn't he refuse to see you?" said he.

"No; he refused to see poor Mr. Dennison." Ruth used the slighting pity of the successful. "We didn't try to go to him; we went to his wife."

Amos sat down. "Ruth," he said, solemnly, "you haven't got talent, you've got genius!"

"Why, of course," said Ruth, "he might snub us and not listen to us, but he would have to listen to his wife. She is such a pretty lady, Amos, and so kind. We had a little bit of trouble seeing her at first, because the girl (who was all dressed up, like the pictures, in a black dress and white collar and cuffs and the nicest long apron), she said that we couldn't come in, the Governor's wife was engaged, and they were going out of town that day. But when Elly began to talk to her she sympathized at once, and she got the Governor's wife down. Then I told her all about Sol and how good he was, and I cried and Elly cried and *she* cried—we all cried—and she said that I should see the Governor, and gave us tea. She was as kind as possible. And when the Governor came I told him everything about Sol—about his mother and the little boy at the mill and the dog, and how he saved the other boy, pulling out that big iron bar red-hot—"

"But," interrupted Amos, who would have been literal on his death-bed—"but it wasn't a very big bar. Not the bar they begin with—a finished bar, just ready for the shears."

"Never mind ; it was big when I told it, and I assure you it impressed the Governor. He got up and walked the floor, and then Elly threw herself on her knees before him ; and he pulled her up, and, don't you know, not exactly laughed, but something like it. 'I can't make out,' said he, 'from your description much about the guilt or innocence of Solomon Joscelyn, but one thing is plain, that he is too good a fellow to be hanged !'"

"And did you take the dagger I sent, and my telegram ?"

"Your telegram ? Dagger ? Amos, I'm so

sorry, but we didn't go back to our lodgings at all. We had our bags with us, and came right from the Governor's here !"

"Then you didn't say anything about evidence ?"

"Evidence ?" Ruth looked distressed. "Oh, Amos! I forgot all about it !"

Amos always supposed that he must have been beside himself, for he caught her hand and kissed it, and cried, "You darling !" Nothing more, not a word ; and he went abjectly down on his knees before her chair and apologized, until, frightened by her silence, he looked up— and saw Ruth's eyes.

After all, the evidence was not at all wasted ; for the Italian woman, thanks to a cunning use of the dagger, made a full confession ; and, the public wrath having been sated on Sol, a more merciful jury sent the real assassin to a lunatic asylum, which pleased Amos, who was not certain whether he had not stepped from one hot box into another. Ruth told Amos, when he asked her the inevitable question of the lover, "I don't know when exactly, dear, but I think I began to love you when I saw you cry ; and I was *sure* of it when I found I could help you !"

Honest Amos did not analyze his wife's heart ;

he was content to accept her affection as the gift of God and her, and his gratitude included Sol and Elly ; wherefore it comes to pass that a certain iron-worker, on a certain day in December, always dines with Amos Wickliff, his wife, and Mother Smith. Amos is no longer sheriff, but a citizen of substance and of higher office, and they live in what Mother Smith fears is almost sinful luxury ; and on this day there will be served a dinner yielding not to Christmas itself in state ; and after dinner the rougher will rise, his wineglass in hand. "To our wives!" he will say, solemnly.

And Amos, as solemnly, will repeat the toast : "To our wives! Thank God!"

THE END

www.ingramcontent.com/pod-product-compliance
Lightning Source LLC
Chambersburg PA
CBHW030630030726
47497CB00006B/1715